The Unknown
An Anthology

William Gillespie
Frank Marquardt, Scott Rettberg
& Dirk Stratton

SPINELESS BOOKS URBANA, ILLINOIS

Contents

MCCARTHY	1	ATLANTA	41
L.A. (AUSTER)	2	LIKE	44
WILL	3	FRANK SLEEPS	48
TRIP	4	ALBUQUERQUE	51
AMERICA	5	OPEN ROAD	53
JUKEBOX	6	APPALACHIA	54
UNKNOWN	8	AWARDS	55
INNOCENT	9	BEAR	57
IRONY	10	THE BOOK OF SIGNS	59
I74	11	FRANK SPEAKS 2	65
HYPERTEXT	12	ON HEROIN	66
LOVE	13	GENIUS	67
LOVE 2	14	PLANE TO FRANCE	69
IOWA	15	PARIS FRANK	71
MAINE	19	PORTLAND	74
ARTICULATION	22	UC-DAVIS	78
TRAVEL	23	I.E.	80
UP NORTH	24		
BROWNU	26	THE BLAND TASTE	81
BROWN RESOLVE	30		
TEXAS	31	H.G. WELLS	101
1999	32	IN ORBIT	102
SEATTLE 2	33	DIRK SPIRIT	103
SEATTLE	35	TIME	106
SAN FRAN FRANK	36	CORTAZAR	107
SOUTH	39	ANGELS	108

UNKNOWN CLUB 3	109	LITIGATION	190
BUNGIE	110	MONTANA	191
L.A. (AUSTER) 2	113	NEBRASKA	195
L.A. (AUSTER) 3	115	NEW OFFICE	200
BOSTON	119	OKLAHOMA	202
BULLSHIT	124	OUT OF JAIL	204
SOCIALISTS	125	EIGHTIES	205
SPECIAL WAY	126	PLAYBOY	206
ALASKA	127	PINSKY	210
BERNHARD ORANGE COUNTY	128	RHYME	211
ROCKIES	129	RITUAL	215
COLORADO	130	RUSTY	216
COURTROOM	136	STOCK CRASH	220
DC	139	VIENNA	223
DENVER	152	XMAS	224
DETAILS OF WHICH	153	LAPD	228
DENOUEMENT	154	INSOMNIA	230
DIRK	156	M.E.	231
DISC GOLF	157	L.A. DIRK DEATH	233
FBI FILE	173	READER	240
000912	177		
FRANK SPEAKS	179	CYBERTEXT, COLLABORATION,	
POOLGAME	181	AND THE BEATLES (TAKE 10)	243
HARD CODE 8	184		
TAIN	186		
ISRAEL	188		

Every so often four writers come along who, it is obvious from the very beginning, are destined for greatness. They are great before anybody knows them, possibly the instant they are born. Read this book: The Unknown. *It is the newest, latest, hippest, youngest, freshest, most happening, best, most outrageous, most intense and in a certain sense the most significant young prose in America: witheringly funny, grotesquely comprehensive, grimly smart, and so wrenching as to be moving, infinitely readable, a grand monstrous powerful thing, shadowy yet redemptive, unreflectively entangled in crimes of demarcation, original and audacious, a vast comic epic and a study of the postmodern condition, hilarious, appalling, moving, subtle, wise, gritty, precisionist, enigmatic, and in this book lifelong themes of love and anger, family politics, sexuality, and the body of the city can be seen gathering in power and clarity, and it develops a freedom and psychic energy born triumphantly of well-wrought pain and determination, all in a new architecture, a wholly new voice, and even a new chemistry of words and images. Two thumbs up.*

—Arthur C. Danto, *The New Yorker*

Everybody gets told to write about what they know. The trouble with many of us is that at the earlier stages of life we think we know everything—or to put it more usefully, we are often unaware of the scope and structure of our ignorance. Ignorance is not just a blank space on a person's mental map. It has contours and coherence, and for all I know rules of operation as well.

—Thomas Pynchon, *Slow Learner*

In June, 1998, Thomas Pynchon's opening epigram in the hypertext novel The Unknown resounded like a rifle-shot from computers across the world and announced a literary revolution. The Unknown had redefined the lyric parameters of popular literature, demonstrating that the seemingly cold hypertext idiom could express the most sophisticated and ambiguous emotions. But this was something else—this was a rock record. It was not a two-minute-and-thirteen second rock and roll single, it wasn't about dancing or driving or teenage love lost and found. This was an electric epic, simple in its sentence-structure but remarkably complex and ambitious in its scope. Its length, subject matter, and medium were totally at odds with what constitutes a hit single.

First, it clocked in at a gargantuan five hundred pages, easily twice as long as a readable hypertext novel was meant to be. It was also lyrically daunting, defying all attempts to fix its precise storyline, yet arresting in its coupling of a childish malevolence with a sense of pain and disillusionment far more adult than anything normally read on a website.

—Fred Goodman, from *The Hotel on the Hill: Gillespie, Rettberg, Stratton, and the Head-on Collision of Literature and Commerce*

Dear friend, now when a flood of paper comes to rest in explicable stacks across campus. Now when sighing library workers face mountains of unshelved books stretching to the ceiling, the majority of the patrons dissipated for intersession. Now when overflowing blue recycling receptacles are turned to by weary janitorial staff. Now when a haze of text clears and you stand looking down at cars in need of repair, dirty floors, the soulless utility of your temporary lodgings here against the bewildering impoverished razed prairies and agricultural blight beyond. And knowing that this bridge of theory will collapse the moment any water flows beneath it. Flowing towards the debts that channel deep underground into hissing sulfur caverns. You fold your diploma into a tiny boat, set it in the current, and, very gently, try to step inside.

Toward the end of the Millennium, we had published a book of our best writing and we traveled the world to promote it. We were generally reckless and lucky, and the whole undertaking proved to be very successful. We had done, we felt, good work, and we deserved to live our dream. Then, after we returned from China, we were offered the opportunity to write a motion picture, and so we moved to Los Angeles.

What then happened has been documented elsewhere, but the point is that fame and wealth very nearly destroyed us: before the end, one of us had died, another had a kind of epiphany, and I had become the sworn enemy of a number of people who used to find me quite likeable.

Where the story begins is that we're creative writers. We write books. We can't help it. It is arguably not our fault that this is the only thing we are good at. So imagine getting this job: creative writer. And you go to the address and then you discover that it's a haunted, decrepit mansion. It's a really unpleasant place and there are ghosts, none of whom will tell you what your job responsibilities are. They shriek at you and recite T.S. Eliot. It's like this haunted mansion is so bad, the ghosts don't even know why they haunt it. And your job is to go there and die, to die hunched at a desk with a machine, by killing yourself slowly, and smearing your every drop of blood over so many miles of clean white pages, ruining them forever. And you call your parents and you tell them that you got a job.

So now it was the three of us driving to Seattle. Our book tour. We had seen an opportunity and we had made it ours. We had built a literature, crammed it into a van, and we were heading for the Rockies. Laptop in lap, writing our third Unknown anthology—our anthology of travel memoirs, written on the tour of the first two books: *The Unknown: An Anthology*, and *The Unknown: Criticism*, a book of essays written by us about our first book. Technological advances had cut out the middleman between writer and readers—in effect eliminating the whole publishing industry. We were a celebration of that. And we were in a van looking for a campgound. I was in the back asleep dreaming of our fourth Unknown anthology: *The Unknown: Cookbook*.

But there had been a flat tire. I sat up and stared at an American landscape we had not yet named, as the car wobbled to rest beside the road.

Dirk had been driving while Scott typed. I had fallen alseep in the middle of a hallucination and was unsure what was. "Where are we?" I asked. "I don't know," said Dirk. "I know," said Scott, typing. But he wouldn't tell us. I climbed out of the back of the van and looked around.

I realized that the tire needed to be changed and that the three of us, collectively, being academic professionals (not to mention the Hope of America), working together with the blaze of charisma and virtuosity that had so captivated our reading public, didn't know how to change a tire.

And the irony of this, it seemed then, against that mountainscape, invited us to drink and to write volumes. So on that deserted road with that sunset and that flat tire, we took turns writing on Scott's laptop. And we wrote so well that nobody would ever again need Homer.

We had set out to find America. The rugged expanse of which is impossible to describe. Which we will most definitely have to describe:

Imagine, if you will, a shapely woman. She is shaped like a continent, and instead of edges, she has shores. And her shores are sandy. There are starfish nearby, picture them, there are fifty of them and they are white against a blue backdrop. In her pubes there is marijuana. And beneath her left arm oil refineries. They are shapely and cast an indigo glow. She is waiting for you to visit her, on a boat docking on her left elbow, and she has forms for you to fill out, yes, lots of them, and there are laws, lots of them, laws you can never understand because they are written in a language you have difficulties with, in a style that even those who know the language have difficulties with. It is like trying to change a tire when you were trying to invent a new wheel, a wheel nobody knew they had always needed because they hadn't thought of it yet, a literature. Which is like an insect. But within her there are taxicabs and restaurants featuring the foods of countries with better food, and there is the exciting sense that nobody here has figured out what they are doing here, and you could be one of the lucky few who is the first to know what she is doing. And in such a strange country. But these people, as crude as they no doubt seem, have a literature. And since it is all they have, they take it seriously.

We only wanted to be a literature jukebox; something you could return to.

You would always go back to that same lonely URL and punch the same numbers and hear the same stories.

After a couple of drinks you might laugh or cry.

The canon should have been that way, but we wanted to be something you might feed quarters, like a literary pinball machine, a game of chance, a practice.

We could have been like a literature trivial pursuit with six narratives, each packed with trivia.

The game of life, something you could take your kids along with you on, as long as you covered their eyes at some points.

We wanted to be a wine joint with candleflames dancing in Chianti bottles—you could crawl into a table in the corner along the vertices of a web of darkness, like a spider.

With always the same folksinger in the corner.

We would light up and make noises, there would be fragments of pleasing, familiar music, and the sequence would never repeat.

Like every time you went to the bar for another pint of beer it was a different bar with different beers on tap. It was the habit you could never repeat.

And thus Unknown were we, wanting to draw a bar room full of readers on through the fog, lit by cigarettes, somehow curious and relieved.

And well you might have thought, if novels are the wood, the deeply grained, stained, palmed, oiled, wiped wood of this bar, then those four, three, five, howevermany Unknown were the neon in the window.

Something in the darkness and smoke of the web, where they always charged too little and poured too high, a tavern of love.

When you get right down to it, it's all sublime. That is, indescribable. You don't stop, though. You keep trying to describe it.

Language games become a form of breathing.

What you don't know can and will hurt you, but not as much as what you already know, which already has and will continue to bring you pain.

This is also the ultimate cause of joy.

To what extent is the unknown a function of memory, and to what extent fate?

We are frontier-obsessed creatures. From America, could we be otherwise? This is not all the stuff of domination. One would hope. To know what is not known. This is the limit and the expanse and the ultimate undoing of all horizons.

But how can we explore the spaces between understandings of things? How can we begin to question how we remember, not what we remember?

How can we know the totality of what we do not think?

There is a problem of scale. To discuss U.S. foreign policy is to avoid discussion of the fact that we are sitting at a table.

There is a problem of etiquette. That is, in addition to the Unknown, there is the Undiscussed. And we are sitting at a table. But that fact is not very interesting to us right now.

No one would ever describe our time in the Midwest as insane, or as decadent. That was the beginning, that first road trip, when we were still truly and completely unknown, aside from the hypertext. Weeks later, we would remember that time as one of innocence, as one of hunger. There was fire in our bellies and we were looking for readers. Our budget was shoestring, and our ride was not luxurious. We had to rely on friends, old teachers, people we knew tangentially, for food and places to crash. But we made every appearance, in those early days, just as scheduled, by hook and crook, fixing breakdowns with duct tape, fixing bored miles of corn with word games and laughter. We didn't know how we would make it from one day to the next. A bowl of ramen and a six-pack of Bud was a kingly feast back then. We had to be creative with our time, not knowing what would come, relying on words for our sustenance. How I long for those days of disorder, of hunger, of facing down the unknown!

We had seen the violence that is beer, we had seen that firsthand, and we had lined up to order pitchers of that violence. And we had done research. Lots. And we weren't about to start citing sources. We were creative writers. And we lied and stole and we called each other at home and demanded beer or text or both, naming brands and degrees Fahrenheit, and our expectations in terms of plot and point of view.

We had stopped looking for ironies when we realized that we were in fact living them.

We left Champaign-Urbana by 6: brewed coffee, said goodbye to my cats, filled up at the Clark station on Cunningham, and hit I-74 West with the orange sun burning a promise in the rearview mirror. Dirk slid a Sweet Honey in the Rock tape into the dash and rolled up a number of truly Mexican proportions. We knew we would have to conserve, but at the outset the euphoria was inescapable. As the vocal quartet sang about Reagan sending troops to Central America, we passed, with relish and satisfaction, and smiled. And we understood that we were all happy. We were going to Normal, we were going to see Curt White, we were going to Alaska, and we were going to find Frank Marquardt. Dirk and Scott had framed their Ph.D.s and those frames were mounted on the dash. My M.S. we used to roll up the next number and we slid through the corn past Farmer City singing smiling and passing.

Hypertext, to put it clearly, is a mapping of a text onto a four-dimensional "space." Normal grammars, then, do not apply, and become branching structures anew. Fragments, branches, links.

The word is glowing and on a screen. It is electronic and cannot be touched. It has been copied over thousands of times and reverberates through virtual space. The text coils in on itself, it is a topographic map of the air currents in the upper atmosphere: those sudden winds that change direction inexplicably.

The reader becomes a sort of satellite taking photographs of a huge and varied terrain. The reader can see the whole world or zoom in to see a particular ant on the banks of the Seine. The ant has six legs. The reader is staring at a video screen. How then, to turn the page? There is no paper.

It is, as Borges might write, a "library of Babel" in which there are so many books all in one place that one is tempted not to read at all.

In the early stages, you call your answering machine, even though it's too late to return any calls, hoping to hear her voice, so that you can now begin agonizing over being unable to return the call, how the agony seems so profound, how—in truth—it is profound, how love is the greatest narrative, how sad it is that we too often let the profound become lost, how we forget the giddiness of sharing the stories of our "irrational" behavior concerning our soon-to-be (i.e. professed, finally) loved one, how that giddiness in metafiction fuels the erotics, the longing, the desperate pull toward a body too recently, reluctantly, abandoned.

But that's not all.

There's more, always more, of love and truth.

There's when you look at yourself in the mirror. It can be a physical mirror and it can be the mirror in your head and it can be a pane of glass and it can be a puddle after weeks of rain. You think, that wasn't love, or that was love, or that is lost love, or I'll never feel that way again, or I wish I could do it over again even though it hurt me motherfucking hurt me, or let me call this beloved, let me call that beloved, or what I wouldn't do to feel again, or... It gets harder as you age, one beloved said to another beloved, it gets harder; but as one ages it becomes easier, too, to say that yes, I feel, I feel. So which is it? Harder or easier or neither or both? For who and for whom and for who? This was love, a story: she met him at the end of her life and died not in his arms—that is how it used to happen, it doesn't happen like this today—but watching the path that he'd walk to reach her, she could almost see him when it happened. Love invites truth, it invites the profound, but this isn't what it is. This isn't it. This isn't love. It's too easy to conflate love with the truth, with the profound. Love is something different though and we hope it's here, somewhere, in this story, this narrative, this place. Because for what else would we do this? From where else would this come? What have we titled this place, the home to these words, to the other words, to some small piece of some small person's time, some group of persons laboring individually apart mostly and without the time or the time-machine or the space-machine to be all there forever, as in our infant stages we wish to live, one supposes, pre-pregnancy, pre-birth? Here is the pain. The small things that take you from now to now, the small things that you enjoy, the short bicycle ride, the butterfly, the cat on your lap, whatever it is, this is of what we try to speak. All titles are really of one. Life is but an exploded nexus of being unimaginable and so is love.

And so we had read at Prairie Lights, where I had bought my first copy of *Writer's Market* when I was 19 years old. And so it had gone well, more or less. There had been some gnashing of teeth. William had been accosted by a crowd of young M.F.A.-getting poets who said that language poetry was not allowed, and in response he had read *Table of Forms*, or anyway part of it. Coover had appeared to be amused, at least enough that he refused to sign any autographs while we were reading. There was some tension in the room, sure, but as long as Coover was happy, we were happy.

Frank Conroy was already drunk. Dirk had already vomited, as usual, and then read haiku. I think it was peyote, this time. I apologized to Conroy about a piece Krass-Mueller had written about him, which had seemed to me to be cruel. Krass-Mueller's piece was about how Conroy wrote a travel piece for some cruise line. This was in Krass-Mueller's piece, which was ripping on cruise lines, for *Harper's*, who sent him on a cruise, which he did not enjoy. It was a funny piece, but I thought it was kind of cruel to rip on Conroy when Conroy was just doing the kind of thing that we (I mean writers, you know?) all do when we're hard up for cash. I mean we (The Unknown) had already done shit that was far worse than that. For cold hard cash. For the Almighty Dollar. We were prostituting ourselves for the sake of American literature, and I told him that our friend Frank had even written copy for Procter & Gamble. Writers gotta eat, I said to him, and fuck, if you can get on a cruise for free, you get to eat, which is part of the job, right? Or at least it comes with the territory. I told him about some fucking intern at *Harper's* who'd pissed me off once when I sent them a story. But he didn't piss me off so much that we'd turn down the opportunity to publish excerpts of our travel memoirs in said magazine. I mean I don't hold a grudge, you know? Of course later, we'd blow that opportunity, too, when we missed our dinner with Lapham. But this was all before that ugly night in Boston. This night was special. I wasn't even on heroin at the time.

And so we had read at Prairie Lights. I read some shit I wrote when I was 19 and thought that the best way to get published was to send stuff out to some of the addresses in *Writer's Market*. And don't get me wrong, there's some great people at F&W, and that whole sending stuff out routine works for some people, I've got a lot of friends who've built whole careers like that. And others who've built careers around fucking editors. There I mean fucking in the physical sense. Poets. Whatever works, I guess. But the mail—it's not for me. I mean I tried that once, back when I was 19, back when I still had a pretty good relationship with the U.S. Postal Service. But they had fucked me since then, countless times postal workers had fucked me over. Fuck in the metaphoric sense, I mean, there. Graduate school applications had been lost, magazines had been stolen, and books had never been delivered. So I was supposed to send my shit out into the hands of those fucks? Trust them with my blood, sweat, and tears? I don't think so. So that created some problems. Most publications still don't take email submissions. And even if it got there, I was supposed to trust my work to some pimply-faced fucking intern at *Harper's*? I told Conroy all this, I was kind of babbling, and I told him that that book of his *Stoptime* is a real classic, in my book.

Anyway, the reading was pretty decent, the people in Iowa City just love a decent reading, and we're decent readers. Then we (that is me, Wm., Dirk, Aukema and Coover—Conroy, as I've said, was pretty much wasted by the time the reading started and retired to his room shortly thereafter) went back to Chuck's house and sat in his kitchen and rolled a couple doobies of the Brown University chronic. Coover didn't actually smoke any of it, at least not in front of us. The air was pungent and wholesome.

Coover is, hey let's face it, one of my heroes. So even if he did smoke any, I wouldn't mention it here, because it turns out, we discovered, that a lot of people who read our hypertext novel tend to believe that everything we write about all the highly regarded literary figures who we mention in the hypertext is true. Which, as I've explained, again and again, it's not. It's mostly bullshit, as they say in the vernacular. Still nobody believes me. Like this is some kind of fucking biography. But anyway, I'm not gonna have anybody believing that Coover, who is an American literary icon, a true great man in the "great man" theory of history sense of the word, was actually sitting there getting stoned with us. Regardless.

So we were flying, and then William got lost on Aukema's porch. I should explain. Aukema's porch is a great library. Bookshelves floor to ceiling, chock-full of literature. Almost all of the influences of the Unknown are in there, a lot of them signed. Because Aukema, I should mention this about Aukema, Aukema knows everybody worth knowing who's a writer. Almost. The script to *Taxi Driver*, for instance, was sold over a long distance phone call from the very kitchen we were right then sitting in. T.C. Boyle made Aukema a dwarf character in his novel *World's End*. Aukema is a very cool guy, who, I should mention this right now as a little bonus for all you dissertation-writing types out there, actually had a great deal of influence on the course of late twentieth century American literature. Particularly hypertext literature. Once, I got into a fight, not a real fight, but some pretty serious verbal sparring, in that kitchen of Aukema's with Chris Offut, who thought that my short-short story "Mohawk Hangnail" was dangerous, and that it would be a bad influence on American literature. That it would be bad for the kids. I like Offut's stuff, but we had both been drinking quite a bit of whiskey. I think the word "fuck" was exchanged several times. He might have said "fuck postmodernism," and I might have said "fuck naturalism," but I'm not sure. As I've said, we were both quite drunk. He's a good writer though, check out his book *Kentucky Straight*.

But we were talking about Coover. Have you read *Pricksongs and Descants*, or *A Night at the Movies*, or *Pinocchio in Venice*, or *The Public Burning*? If you haven't read any of his work, I'd recommend that you pop open a window on your browser (yeah, right now, but leave *The Unknown* open, too) and go to your online bookstore of choice and purchase a copy of one of his books. Now, you might not be able to find a few of his books, but I think that most of them are back in print, finally. Which is very good. That it's back in print. His work. Which is good. So let me just come out right now and admit that we've (the Unknown, here referred to collectively) lifted a few techniques from the guy. Is that a crime? I don't think so. Writers can get away with all sorts of that kind of shit. He didn't mind, at any rate, at least that's what he said, when we were sitting in Aukema's kitchen and we admitted to his face that we were ripping him off left and right. And it's not just us I'm talking about either; it's a whole generation of hip American writers. But that's another story. Or is it?

We talked about a lot of things with those two guys, Dirk and me. We talked about molecular biology. We talked about cannibalism and stereotypes of Native Americans. We talked about new medical instruments that are invisible to the naked eye. We talked about evolution. We talked about various pharmaceuticals and how they are tested. We plotted, we schemed, we made big plans for American literature. Hypertext especially. It was a good night, that night in the kitchen at Aukema's house in Iowa City. I think William stole some books from Aukema. I remember thinking that I write an awful lot about marijuana when I am out of it, or some words to that effect.

Crossing the state line into what used to be known as "Vacation-land" depressed Dirk greatly. He had spent six miserable years in Maine during the 1980s and was not pleased at the prospect of returning to the site of his darkest hours.

Felled by a severe migraine that refused to respond to any of the myriad of pharmaceuticals available on the van, Dirk missed the Portland reading entirely. Reports from Marla, who was by now nearly beside herself with fear and grief, indicated that Scott and William had more than made up for Dirk's absence by being even more rude and obnoxious than usual. William alternated between raving about Maine Yankee (Maine's aging and potentially dangerous nuclear reactor) and reprising his "I'm - drifting - into - a - drug - induced - coma - but - don't - request - medical - assistance - or - I'll - make - sure - you - pay - if - and - when - I - recover" act, which was frightening to behold, the way his glazed-over eyes produced hyphen after hyphen to punctuate what amounted to extremely sophisticated drooling. Scott had located some heroin he'd forgotten to use in Seattle and so spent most of the time nodding off, shivering back into semi-consciousness in order to request a beer, then nodding off again. Our manager Marla ended up doing the reading and was repaid for her efforts by being jeered at by her now completely obliterated clients.

By the time the van rolled into Orono, home of Dirk's first graduate school alma mater, the University of Maine, Dirk's migraine had subsided somewhat, due mostly to the frequent full-body massages willingly donated by the coterie of comely disciples who had invited themselves along for the rest of the tour. They drove behind the van and often paid for everybody's meals (though Dirk insisted, out of their earshot, that he did not require such financial contributions, but was unable to say no to such heartwarming generosity). "Right," Scott and William thought, while chowing down on lobster, steak, and clams, liberally doused in Maine Blueberry Syrup.

Both William and Scott had become increasingly concerned about the effect Dirk's cult was having on the book tour. On the one hand, the perks weren't bad, the lobster meals for one, or the occasional make-out session with whichever disciple wasn't chosen to join Dirk as he continued Gandhi's experiment of having naked virgins lie beside him at night to test his vows of chastity. Sure, Dirk's disciples were far from virginal, and the noise levels emanating from Dirk's resting place almost surely belied his claims that he refrained from carnal knowledge, but both Scott and William admired the audacious lying since it reminded them so much of their own work. "Finally," they thought, "Dirk is giving up that effete poetry kind of lying and really laying down some awesome, he-man Hemingway-type of fiction lying." This comforted them, somewhat, though Dirk had seemed to become much more distracted ever since the Tallahassee *Smerz-Transcriber* had published an exposé of Dirk's cult in which they noted that Dirk's school transcripts did not support his declaration that he had been fully trained in clinical hypnosis and transcendental Rolfing. The latter didn't even exist, the Tallahassee paper announced smugly. As if a little thing like credentials could derail Dirk's sacred mission.

Still, both William and Scott agreed that they should keep an eye on their co-author, as well as stop the annoying habit of doing everything in tandem. "They were individuals, dammit!" they shouted loudly, at no one in particular. "Dang, it's happening again! What's with this simultaneous thought, speech, and action Siamese-twin effect?" A sobering thought hit them: perhaps they had been co-opted into Dirk's cult without them even realizing it; perhaps he was at that very moment controlling their lives, putting words in their mouths, even manufacturing the thoughts they were allowed to think. But if that were the case, then even this realization would be the result of Dirk's cruel machinations, a way of starkly revealing the limits of their free will, shining a spotlight on their chains.

After their reading in the University Bookstore, everyone ended up at the Oronoko Restaurant, which specialized in deep-fat fried food. Even the beer was deep-fat fried. At least the reading had gone fairly smoothly. The audience was small, so chances to insult them were reduced. Dirk managed to choke out a couple of poems before the black karma of the place incapacitated him. Scott and William used his limp body as a prop to finish off the evening before returning it to his frantic disciples who began bickering over who would get to perform the first full-body massage.

The articulation is simple. You go through life not knowing. It's like this: You could be this or this. And you are this and this. You live as this and this. The decisions are ultimately arbitrary. They fall into some huge order but how can it be ordered, it's too much to be ordered. It's mutations and DNA and genes and one sperm not another. That's who you are. The product of an infinite impossibility. It's not a jest. And yet you are. So it comes down to this: This point in time. You the you that's you now. But could it be you forever? It would never again be the same. The staggering variations of the rain forest of the human population of the population of rodents thus amounts to what it is. Maybe this is why de Selby said the word *judgement* could not feasibly exist in an unordered or ordered environment regardless of whether or not it was or was not intended by a divine creature. Regardless of the conditions, if this was this was not this or this there could be no word *judgement*. We're wrong to think we know. It's why the wise ones all say they know nothing. Disturbing to think on your last breath everything you did, all you were, was not you. This is what Dirk said. This is how he said it. And we sat watching, eyes rolling into our heads, too drunk to really pay any attention or hear.

There is an ashtray beneath the radio. There may be a map in the glove compartment. I think we missed our turnoff. I will stop and get more coffee. There are empty bottles and wrappers on the floor. I will drive until sunrise and then I will awaken Scott or William. I will then expect to be allowed to sleep in the back seat as I have not had that privilege for some many miles. There is a smell but we are used to it. There are deer on the road and meteors in the night sky.

In Minnesota we got back to nature for three days. Then we got back to the car and drove for three more.

We had had to hike and canoe for two days to get to our reading at the Bookstore in the Woods, a bookstore in the Boundary Waters Canoe Area run year-round by forest rangers. It was in fact the only building in the entire preservation area, but it had been permitted because most hikers had trouble keeping their paperbacks dry. Amazingly, the store sold only books. For the hikers and canoers, carrying freeze-dried food and foraging and fishing were no problem, but the difficulties presented by carrying enough books on two or three-week expeditions, across rivers and through rain and mud, led to an aching desire for literature. The store had a fantastic selection (I bought a Dover Thrift Edition of *Walden*), but only one customer—a mountaineer from Manitoba who had canoed twenty-four days to make it to our reading. We would have given him a copy of the *Anthology*, but of course there was no way we could have carried it two days on our backs through the frequent rain showers.

We had had a great hike. We had had to carry Everclear because it had the lightest weight-per-drink ratio of any available liquor. Many a night we made our freeze-dried split-pea soup with Everclear instead of water; and then we swam, built a fire, passed out, or just gazed at the aurora borealis. It was indescribable. We could never find words to describe it. We just stammered and gaped. No words.

Then we hiked out, found the Winnebago, and made it just in time to our reading at Hungry Mind in St. Paul, Minnesota. We were unshaven, unshowered, and our boots were caked in mud. We hadn't even bothered to remove the canteens of Everclear from our webbed belts. Afterward we had to say goodbye to some very kind admirers and drive all night to get to Shaman Drum Bookshop in Ann Arbor for our noon reading the next day.

We drove straight through. Z was no longer with us, having been arrested for driving under the influence without a license or pants back in Nebraska. So we took turns behind the wheel of the Winnebago, and smoked all Scott's cigarettes.

After the reading in Ann Arbor we left immediately (with no opportunity to meet people and enjoy the city's lax possession laws) to get to Books on the Square Ltd. in Providence for our reading the following afternoon, which was to be followed that night by a very prestigious gig to which we had been looking forward for weeks: Brown University.

Brown was paying us ten thousand dollars and giving us a very large auditorium with a state-of-the-art overhead projector Mac with a T-1 Internet connection, so we could read our hypertext "live" from the Net. They were stocking their bookstores with our books and large color posters of us. Coover was making the reading required for his students in Hypertext 301: Spaces and Fragments.

When we got to Providence, though, extraordinarily exhausted from three days of solid 70+ MPH, a call from Marla on the cellular informed us that the gig at Brown had been canceled because the auditorium had been requested at the last minute by the Kronos Quartet. Kronos had been delighting and outraging their fans this tour by performing the album *Led Zeppelin II* straight through (as arranged for string quartet, theramin, waterdrums, and a variety of original microtonal instruments built by Harry Partch). But Brown was paying us anyway.

So, after our underattended (even for us) reading at Books on the Square, there was nobody from Brown to greet the Unknown in Providence. Sleep-deprived, our discouragement tainted with relief, we had nothing to do for the rest of the day but drink. So we went from the bookstore to the bar across the street—O'Leary's Alehouse—and the four of us—me, Scott, Frank, and William—settled in at a table by the jukebox (which played only Gaelic music) with an ashtray, pretzels, and four pints of a frothy Welsh beer named Schlwtz.

There was an old man at the bar and a man in a suit playing darts alone and a cozy sense that if time passed here, it passed by outside. We each began writing a scene for *The Unknown II: The Time Machine*. (The next day we would have an argument which would lead to us rejecting the time machine idea.)

Scott, on the snappy laptop Marla had bought him for his 30th birthday, began typing his proposal (none of us ever knew if he was serious) for a cable station called UTV: Unknown TV. UTV would feature lavishly-produced text videos in which young poets lip-synched their writing in psychedelic image-processed dramas involving sexy models and sports cars. UTV also featured "Closetcase Classics"—videos of old writing. UTV also featured feature-length movies, such as the powerful biography of Gertrude Stein (Oliver Stone's *Stein*) or Gus Van Sant's *Infinite Jest*. Videos would be introduced by charming young people in designer clothing. There would be concert movies, and literature would be reconciled with the mainstream in a way that would leave the mainstream fond of literature while literature continued to be alienated and wary of the mainstream.

William continued working on *The Unknown: Crossword Puzzle*. It was a poetry project based on a list of 100 constraints, which operated simultaneously across two languages. He had had to learn French and C++ in order to write the code to search the OED online to find the words. He had been working on it for a year. Nobody else really approved of the project but they knew better than to criticize it. And the mood at O'Leary's was good. In that dank warmth, the idea of a crossword puzzle written in Alexandrines without the letter E or five-letter words made sense, and was even worthy of a toast or three.

Frank wrote a scene about how, around the year 2010, the Unknown had a reunion concert at Carnegie Hall. A lot of our old fans and friends had paid 100 bucks a ticket and there was a certain tension. Our old fans weren't crazy about our newer stuff. We were reading our latest hypertext novel—*The Unknown: Suburbs*—about how four writers named Scott, Frank, Dirk, and William all got married and moved into a gated community together.

Half of the crowd was trying to boo us off the stage. They didn't properly appreciate the depth of the scene with Frank in AA, nor the scene with Scott borrowing Dirk's lawnmower, nor the scene with William pushing his daughter on the swingset and telling her about insurance copayments.

I was writing about Unknownpalooza—the Unknown's outdoor rock concert. We gave seven readings and between them different bands would play. It was weird because we were the oldest people there and we had never heard of any of the bands. But the kids loved us, and by the end of the concert I had dreadlocks, and Scott had a nose ring and a pierced lip. William wanted to get a tattoo of Gaddis on his back, but the tattoo artist, who claimed to be able to do any tattoo, had never heard of Gaddis and was apologetic but uninterested.

We were all writing and chuckling and drinking and eating pretzels when the man in the suit stopped playing darts and pulled up a chair at our table. He had recognized us.

He introduced himself as John Tormey III. He was an entertainment, art, and media lawyer who handled transactional matters, as well as certain claims and litigation matters as they pertain to the entertainment business. He told us about his Martindale-Hubbell lawyer's rating, as well as his timely and responsive representation of his clients. He had studied at Harvard and at the UCLA School of Law.

We were all very impressed. We had a certain detached admiration for those who had gone to college in order to obtain marketable skills. There ensued much backslapping and handshaking and roundbuying. Tormey told us stories about U2, Negativland, and Casey Kasem; we told him about Krass-Mueller. Just by way of fucking with the man, Frank posed an interesting hypothetical legal case:

"Say a man has been, using email, helping to write a hypertext novel, and has been given little in the way of editorial power. Say that the man no longer wants to write the hypertext novel, and wants all his writing excised from the novel so that he might publish those scenes elsewhere, or incorporate them into different print novels composed by him alone. Then there ensues disagreement between the four or more collaborating authors as to which of the various parties actually wrote what. Because many of the scenes were written together; or written by one person and edited by another, and proofread by another; were written under the influence or over telnet; the disagreements are very complicated indeed. Say, for example, that there is a very heated argument over whose property is the soft-core porn art-poem 'Still Life with My Pecker,' or 'Somebody's Always Fucking with My Mirrors'... Say the man hires you. How do you proceed?"

But we never got to hear his opinion because at that point Robert Coover, the Kronos Quartet, and a gaggle of Brown faculty entered the bar. Carole Maso was buying everyone drinks. Gale Nelson winked at us, and put a five-dollar bill into the jukebox.

It looked like we might get to have fun in Providence after all.

At Brown, the Unknown resolved to save hypertext from the academy: too much scrutiny inevitably makes one want to scatter to dark corners to escape the light, to avoid being the object of obsessive voyeurism, which scholarship inevitably tends to emulate. How difficult it becomes to be watched while working: one begins watching oneself being watched and while watching the watching one loses the work or it becomes about all the watching going on. It's a pyramid scheme, and not enough audience to go around. Who will watch the watchers?

After our reading at The Twig Bookshop in San Antonio, a mute woman smiled and passed us a cryptic note as we signed the *Anthology* three times. A meeting had been arranged.

We found the old man in a shack near the Mexican border working on an old Underwood. When we tapped at the door he squinted through the curtain and knew who we were. He took us to his barn. It was a long walk across the desert. Saguaro cacti bent against the wind-driven sands. He told us: "This is where Pynchon wrote most of *Gravity's Rainbow*." He reached up onto a rafter, causing a lizard to scurry out of hiding, and he brought down a tiny vial. He squeezed a drop of clear liquid onto his hand. Then Dirk's. Scott said no. Then mine. The vial was crystalline and a shaft of sunlight ricocheted tiny rainbows. I heard a little girl laughing distant yet close by. I observed that the wood was melting. I was laughing and felt tears on my cheeks. We sat in the barn and could not leave because the sunlight outside was too bright. Then I noticed the first tarantula. The old man laughed. His face was like a peanut. He was withered and every line he had written was somewhere etched into his face. It grew dark. There was a squeaking I took to be bats. The old man lit a gas lantern, which whooshed, and he unfolded a starchart. He told us something about Betelgeuse and he took a bottle of whiskey out of a desk drawer and we went out to look up into the Texas night. What we saw there I will never understand or forget.

The majority of the book tour actually took place during the summer and fall of 1999.

Too often that year, we took the advice of The Artist Formerly Known as Prince, and partied like it was 1999. Which it was. But which, in retrospect, was mostly just a convenient excuse for all that excess. The nation was going crazy. Al Gore was campaigning against Daryl Gates, former head of the LAPD. The Y2K countdown was affecting people in weird ways. Those predisposed to believe in apocalypse were sure it was coming. When enough people are convinced that the world is ending, the world might as well be ending.

As for us, we believed in no such thing; we were cutting our feet on the bleeding edge of the next American literature. Our hypertext would generate more criticism than Joyce, of this we were convinced. Still, we met a lot of strange people at our readings. Our only concern, which was, at times, overwhelming, was where to spend New Year's Eve. We needed to find the best party in America, and we had to start looking in July.

"Good to be home,"

Dirk sighed, as the van lumbered down First Avenue towards Pioneer Square. It was a postcard type of day; Mt. Rainier loomed ahead, free of the clouds that usually hid it and its volcanic destiny, i.e., the equivalent of L.A.'s "Big One"—yes, Seattle, once voted Most Liveable City, had an apocalypse of its own disguised cleverly as a placid natural wonder, a snow-capped "oooooooooh"-elicitor for unjaded tourists. Dirk hoped that he could somehow not be in Seattle when Mt. Rainier decided to blow chunks and then return to the city during the aftermath, just before property values recovered. He figured that would be the only way he could ever afford to live in Seattle. He hated the idea of profiting from others' misfortune, but on the other hand, he had been raised an American and so took a certain glee in imagining a real estate coup akin to when John D. Rockefeller used the 1929 Crash to fill his portfolio with oodles of price-challenged stocks. "I've got to cut back on the weed smoking," Dirk thought. He could barely afford a pair of jeans these days; where would he get the capital to become a real estate mogul in a post-Rainier era? Time enough to solve that conundrum. Now he had but two goals: get through their reading at Eliot Bay Books and score some fine Pacific Northwest sativa. The former would prove to be the most difficult.

William precipitated the crisis when, after ingesting far too many Budweiser and Nyquil cocktails, he began calling the store the Effete Fey Kookstore, and yelling loudly that he owned more poetry than anyone in the place and he had a database file on a floppy to prove it. The staff, the usual collection of aging hippies and school librarians on crank, were as gracious as they could be given the circumstances, but when William insisted that it be collected poems at dawn, 20 paces, and began loudly demanding a one-volume edition of Robert Kelly's complete works to serve as his weapon of choice, the night manager pulled Scott aside and softly suggested we put a muzzle on William pronto or kiss the reading goodbye. Whatever else Seattle may be, it's a good book town, so a chance to face such a potentially receptive audience was not something to cavalierly toss aside, despite William's apparent move to do so. While Scott distracted William, I snuck up behind him carrying an *American Heritage Dictionary*. William's skull responded well to the healthy crack I delivered to his raving head and he dropped soundlessly to the floor. We immobilized him with packing tape and propped him up on stage for the duration of our presentation. Occasionally, we would nod in his direction and he would begin writhing; flecks of spittle sometimes slipped passed the adhesive and formed a small pool in his lap.

We nearly broke up the tour that fateful evening in Seattle. That it had come to this…this violence…and words were exchanged that…that pretty much brought Scott to tears. He left the bookstore after reading some of William's poems and walked off alone with the van keys in his pocket. He knew Dirk would find someplace to crash, and that he could probably take William with him.

Scott did heroin and had a double latté. On the street it was rainy and he stood there in a trench coat and a hat with a brim. He lit a cigarette and thought about the text, and the sign, and the rest of us. What was nagging at him right then was the realization that he didn't know what Postmodernism actually was, nor would he ever. And yet he considered himself a scholar through and through, of the highest caliber. He had to walk for a while. He walked over a bridge and down a street. There was rain and water on the ground. The cement was shiny. Each fiber of cigarette smoke was brought to color by neon. There was the smell of fresh fish and the sounds of Chinese language. Postmodernism, of all the fucking things, why did he need to worry about that now, when he almost had everything he wanted.

"Postmodernism."

He thought.

I are media.

We is media.

There was no Yoko to blame, no war that would separate, no employment situation which could pull apart this intrepid band. But the road had taken its toll. Dirk had taken to wearing a hempen robe. William had developed a nasty habit of getting into fist-fights with other writers named William. It happened at nearly every stop on the tour. And Scott couldn't believe in po-mo no mo. Later, he found the boys crashed on top of the van. Which was locked. No words were exchanged. But the forgiveness was palpable. They got in the van and headed to San Francisco.

Hell, it doesn't matter, Dirk, Scott, and William, three guys these are guys. I've got a bottle of malt liquor in a brown paper bag and a pocketful of alfalfa sprouts and I say to Scott, buddy, what can we cook up with this? He says, cookbooks, cookbooks. He's not talking real straight at this point, has been thinking he's the Oracle at Delphi or else the Oracle at Oracle, I couldn't tell which, because he'd say one word and repeat it as if it meant more repeated. Cookbooks, cookbooks, he says, and we go to cookbooks and I start looking in James Beard and Julia Child for alfalfa sprouts and Scott takes the same books and checks the index for beer. Alfalfa, Scott says, alfalfa, like it's supposed to mean something. Then I get this badass idea because I'm feeling around in my back pocket and there's a Hershey bar there. Chocolate, I say to Scott, chocolate. Think of a cauldron of chocolate and you're drinking beer in it and you're eating alfalfa sprouts. He vomits all over Julia Child.

This happened at Borders. We got all turned around earlier, because I told the taxi driver or whoever it was whose car we were in—I think it was a German tourist, on reflection—we needed City Lights and he said, uh?, and I said, bookstore, and he doesn't get it, so we're at Borders. But we need to be at City Lights, the next S. Burroughs was reading and I was giving the introduction, so I pick Scott up and carry him out of the store. People were looking but fuck them. Adios, Scott says, adios. Clap, Scott says, clap.

I carry him to City Lights. It's a long ways and he vomits in my back pocket on the way, but so what, I'm drunk. We get to City Lights and the next S. Burroughs, that's William, is standing up in front of a huge crowd of people. He's just standing there. William, I whisper, after dropping Scott in the poetry room, what are you doing? He looks at me. It's this mind-reading trick he learned in Dirk's cult, I think. Dirk's telepathic, I think. Who knows? Whatever, I realize William's saying to me, I can't talk until I've been introduced. Now, if you know William, you know he's a man of few words even when he does talk. I ask somebody in the audience, how long has this been going on? And this person in the audience vomits. Now, this confused me. Because Scott just vomited. But then it occurs to me Dirk's into peyote. He loves peyote. And it occurs to me further that William is on peyote, too. And it occurs to me further that me, I'm on it too, and I might vomit soon. But first I should introduce William as the next S. Burroughs, because that's who—and I see this clearly at the time, as if I am the Oracle—he is. So I go up in front of everybody, work my jaw a bit but don't say anything, and then say—I don't say anything. I think it. And now, I think, William, the next S. Burroughs, is going to read from his novelette, his collection of poetry. He's going to read from his experimental novel and his conventional one. He's going to read from his thesis and he's going to read from his students' papers.

At this point Scott meanders in. He's not saying anything, but he's thinking something. Ode, he thinks, ode. He sits in the single empty chair in the back next to the books on astrology and stops thinking, empties his mind, becomes Zen. Then Dirk comes in with about 100 disciples, I don't know how many there were, but they're all wearing this shirt that's got a picture of a bald Dirk on the front of it and on the back the words, "Olean," so I think immediately that Procter & Gamble is sponsoring this cult, and sure enough, under "Olean" it reads: "P&G: For the best in anal leakage." Crowd, I think, here is the allegedly arisen one. Everyone nods their head.

Inexplicably, the lights go out. City Lights is dark like the Dead Sea after the apocalypse.

I pause, and then continue thinking: William's going to read from his term papers, I think, he's going to read from his class notes, he's going to read from cereal boxes and from grocery store coupons. He's going to read fortune cookie fortunes, underwear size labels, text from highway billboards, the *Declaration of Independence*, the script to *Goodfellas*, the warning label on the back of a container of antifreeze, and James Beard cookbooks. He's going to read transcripts of conversations with Curtis White, Scott Rettberg, myself, and Dirk; he's going to read auras; he's going to read tea leaves and street addresses and calling card access codes and the *Wall Street Journal Guide to Understanding Money and Investing* and *Funk & Wagnall's Encyclopedia* and the sports page of a Brazilian newspaper and God in a clump of Dirk's hair. And you know what, I think. And he's also going to read my mind. Everybody applauds him, as S. Burroughs begins to read.

Aside from a quick trip to Tampa to douse an already dormant romance that barely got past the flint-and-steel-spark phase (with a little oral sex thrown in to make things confusing), and a trip to Atlanta for an AWP meeting, Dirk had never visited the South, nor did he know much about it. Oh, he had the usual distortions firmly in place, supplied by TV and movies, *Dukes of Hazzard, Deliverance, Cool Hand Luke,* and the like. Add to those the usual prejudices common to non-Southerners and you will not be surprised to learn that Dirk was apprehensive about this leg of the journey, particularly since the book tour seemed to be fueled by a pharmacy of drugs, that is, if pharmacies sold illegal drugs. Dirk's dreams all turned to nightmares as Dixie began to loom and all his nightmares contained a corpulent cop, a Bull Connors-clone, who liked to use his nightstick to perform cavity searches. Upon hearing about these dreams, Scott accused Dirk of harboring latent homophobia. "Suck tailpipe," Dirk pleasantly countered, as he began to destroy as much evidence of illegal activity as possible by ingesting it. "Hey, save some for the rest of us," William cried in alarm.

Scott shut off the alarm and began to massage his left calf which had a surplus of lactic acid interfering with his normal leg extension capability. Dirk's secret fear was that he would begin unconsciously adopting a Southern accent and thereby inadvertently insult the natives. He wasn't sure why a Southern leg was even necessary, since his prejudices included the notion that none south of the Mason-Dixon line had earned a high school diploma, which meant that the potential market for an overly-educated project such as theirs would have to be practically nil.

Later, Dirk recalled just how little he recalled of the South. "I'll have to visit again, I guess," he told himself, once he sobered up. Of the little he could remember, the event that stood out in his mind was a reading in Austin, Texas. Or rather, the party after the reading. In an attempt to ingratiate himself with a prominent poet who was a member of the faculty at the University of Texas, Dirk began reciting cowboy poetry. He apparently did not do enough to eradicate the sarcasm that suffused his recital, or perhaps it was just his awful imitation of the local accent. In any case, he was told later that if he ever wanted to give up poetry, he really had no future as a boxer, though he might find an opening as a towel somewhere (that is, he had done a pretty good imitation of the aforementioned wiping the proverbial floor). First, Levertov, now a Texas poetry professor. And all this from Saint Dirk: a man so nonviolent, so peaceful, that he called himself Gandhi while showering. He had never been one to believe, as Hemingway apparently had, that besides gripping a pen and a bottle, one's fingers must know how to grip themselves, form a fist, and seek out the soft cartilage of the nose, the glass of the jaw, the solar of the plexus. What was it about the Unknown that made such behavior not only commonplace but seemingly required?

We were generally better behaved in New Orleans.

What happened in Atlanta was that a very polite man in a chauffeur's uniform met us after our reading at A Capella Books in Little 5 Points and whisked us cross-state. A few hours later, we were on Ted Turner's yacht off the coast, near Savannah. I don't think Ted trusted us to show. His personal assistant had arranged the meeting with Marla, saying Ted wanted to give us "a look-see."

That was a long boat ride. William got seasick over the side rail. Ted and I talked about Bosnian war crimes. Jane Fonda still looks great. Ted married well. And I don't give a shit what you say about what she was doing during Vietnam. She's a looker and a real good actress with a mind that won't quit.

Frank, awkwardly, kept referring to *Barbarella*. Jane got flushed and embarrassed. Ted scooped her up in his arms tickled and joshed her. They're a real nice couple, always giggling like school-kids.

Ted wanted to do a colorized version of the hypertext, which he would air on the USA Network. But he wanted us to take all the drug references out. We thought it over.

Jane picked up a phone and a butler appeared with a lid of grass.

Jane rolled a joint.

Ted said, "Better be Maui Wowie, son, or you're in the shitter."

The butler said, "But Dad, all I could get was Jamaican."

Jane, sitting cross-legged on the deck in her steel-blue bikini, took a deep hit, and said, "It's good shit, Ted, it's real good."

Ted unhanded the butler, saying, "Dammit, son, when I say Hawaiian, I mean Hawaiian. Jamaica is a whole other island. Am I wastin' my money on all those maps?" He took a big hit and passed the doobie to Dirk, and with a furrowed brow appeared to be weighing matters of substance, then said, "This is good shit, son, so you're lucky. But mark my words, sonny boy, the next time pull something like this, you go right over that rail."

He said all this in a relatively calm, even good-natured, way, so you could tell that he was kidding, but that he was also simultaneously dead serious.

The butler said, "Sorry Dad, it won't happen again."

Ted said, "It had better not. Now go do your homework. Geography and Procurement."

"Yes, Dad," the butler said, and went back below deck, submissively. The waitress then appeared and we had five of the biggest lobsters you've ever seen with drawn butter, and a real nice zucchini, garlic and tomato side dish. We had slushy fruit drinks with Malaysian names. They had mangos and kiwi and pineapple and strawberries in them.

Ted gave us a little talk on the importance of vitamins.

We talked about metaphysics with Jane.

Ted gave us some investment advice.

We didn't do the deal on colorizing the hypertext, but it was a real nice afternoon. The money would have been nice, but at that time we still felt that it was important for us to retain our artistic integrity.

Ted said he'd make sure the book got plugged on CNN.

the unknown is like

a Cargill's Seeds Soil Thermometer
a most versatile item
the thermometer is
built into a flat pointed stick
like a paint-stirring stick
but just a little thicker
the thermometer is embedded
in the stick
the temperature scale
printed on both sides of the wooden slot
so that you can safely jab it
(the Cargill's Seeds Soil Thermometer)
into the damp lush
dirt of your garden
that holds and feeds
your pumpkins lounging
like golden gods after an orgy
that has left them
engorged and comatose
on the far left side
of the Cargill's Seeds Soil Thermometer
is another scale
in inches
so that you can measure the depth

of a snowfall
or a monsoon's worth of rain
or the length of a spider web
or your cat's tail
and given
that the inches scale starts
at zero inches
but the zero
is placed on a line
that has at least an inch
of pointed wood below it
the Cargill's Seeds Soil Thermometer
in a simple
but ultimately profound way
suggests the existence
of negative numbers
numbers that exist only
in the brain
numbers that can't be
physically represented
in the real world
show me −3 apples for example
of course there are those who would retort
all numbers exist
only in the brain

show me a 5
not five things
a 5
you point to the 5
on the Cargill's Seeds Soil Thermometer
that's not a 5
that's the sign for 5
yes but in this case
the sign and the thing
are identical
that's horseshit
and besides you just screwed your own argument
if that's a 5 i don't have to show you −3 apples
just give me some paper
and i'll create a −3
ex nihilo
and you will be astounded
i've always wondered
is horseshit worse than bullshit
it's used less frequently
which would suggest that it is reserved
for those times that demand
a more powerful expletive
and isn't it interesting that we abbreviate

bullshit as b.s.

but we don't abbreviate

horseshit as h.s.

for obvious reasons I guess

since b.s. flows off the tongue

much better than h.s.

and you can say bull and imply

the shit

but you can't do the same with horse

and finally at the top of the stick

a hole

from which to hang

the Cargill's Seeds Soil Thermometer

on a nail

pounded into one of your walls

and bent back just enough to make a hook

so that it

the thermometer not the nail

can perform

yet one more service

recording and displaying

for your sensual pleasure

the current temperature of the air

and that's how it is with the unknown

The future is past, what do you do about that? The secret tonight isn't relevant. It is hidden. You put lime in your beer. What do you want of a night? What do you look for in a woman, what do you look for in a man? The easy answers were taken a long time ago, you realize that. The answers you want to claim for yourself are invalid. So you go out searching. You walk down Mission to Doc's. The drink in your hand isn't the remedy you thought it would be. Later, at the L.A. club, you bump into the pool table, your force knocks a ball in the pocket. Score! That's a winning number nobody had up their sleeves. Keys slide in easily or they challenge you, they fight you. Will you make them work? I don't have your answer. I have words you don't have and these, too, fall far short of saying what you wish had been said. Life hides like dust under a sofa for centuries, or until a family moves, or dies, and there's a reason to look at what was neglected for so long. Hold me! It's Tuesday and I happen to be alone tonight. You will remember this literature you created as one of the great false lies of your life, like a grade you didn't deserve. Nobody will know what you accomplished. It's Tuesday. The week stretches forever. There is Scott holding a camera reminding you of who you are, or who you are not, or who you might one day be. What ambition! What grace holds you, like fluid, in the womb of the life you never wanted, but love, now that you have it. Hold tightly to me. Remember the picture that didn't get developed with the stack you turned in on Tuesday. Tuesday! You wanted this life like nothing. You wanted it like fame. You lie to yourself about your reluctance, but you love what love surrounds you. Give to it. The train won't stand in its stall forever. William is hungry. He reads poetry to himself before bed, as if his desire can be found in the language he doesn't have. Fame costs a fortune, don't forget.

Tomorrow is Saturday.

The density of texts written and unwritten surround you, suddenly, like the call of larks sent from...as if larks were from somewhere sent.

All of the dreams which you have been sent have been sent from yourself to you.

In the end, in the present, you finally realize that all of your fate has been sent by you to you. And you are sloped towards a pillow as you turn off your stereo and begin to contemplate a dream without sleeping as you do every night without sleep but with hope your dream is not without restlessness.

Senseless visions. The stereo still plays. You can't see a thing. The sun won't be out for hours, and when it's out it'll blind you. It's Tuesday. You can't escape the week. You can't escape the responsibility you were given, not given. Who cares? What do you want from time, from music, from music that's time, time that's music. Silence won't speak to you but it will say one word, what it is, a monotony. William, perhaps he sleeps now, perhaps. Dirk's nose hurts, he picks it, it hurts worse. In the present you have days, you have dreams.

Tomorrow is Saturday. Tomorrow.

Saturdays can be dense like sand at the beach. You never know what you've sent or if the postage will carry it the distance you imagined it would traverse.

Restlessness is no more than the sum of its part, like you.

Dirk is dreaming of the Internet and the young man's nose he destroyed in a battle-until-the-end-of-the-finish fight he won whilst trying to woo T.C. Boyle's minions, you remember.

The end of quintessence is essence. The battle is not that and if it was has no point in its fears.

Frank is fighting sleep for fear of what will be written.

Frank will sleep.

Frank is sleeping.

Frank sleeps.

We had given a reading at Books and Coffee, a bookstore whose title speaks of solid integrity, and, as usual, had met some interesting people. I had a headache from the heat and dehydration of the drive and took a pill I thought was ibuprofen. In the middle of my reading I started cracking up. My knees and jaw turned to rubber and I began extemporizing what I thought was a sonnet: "When I get blown in Albuquerque / Get me a Pabst and a stick of beef jerky."

Dirk helped me offstage amid wild applause. I remember the reading he gave seemed like a film sped up. I blinked and then it was over and they were helping me to the car. I had a copy of *Wuthering Heights* I had either bought or stolen or received as a gift and I wasn't sure why.

Then we were at a bar called Two Dollar Bill's. We were with a couple who I remember as a very large man with a beard who spoke little and had a FUCK AUTHORITY t-shirt, and a tiny woman with big hair who talked excessively. She smoked like a demon and she kept giving Scott more cigarettes. They were having Long Island Iced Teas. I think someone ordered me a beer so I'd attract less attention. The place was crowded and there was tension. Dirk and Scott and our two friends went off to throw darts, I think, and I was propped at the bar watching a game on TV. I think it was hockey. I remember a great big Budweiser clock above the bar and the minute hand was moving so quickly I could watch its progression. A giant chipmunk next to me engaged me in conversation. I'm not sure I spoke back or acknowledged him. It didn't matter. He may have taken my wallet. I discovered it was missing the next morning. I woke up in the back seat of the car at dawn, my face flattened against cold glass and sunrise over the Manzano Mountains. There was the remains of a campfire and a tent and Dirk in a sleeping bag on a picnic table. I climbed out of the car and rubbed my limbs, investigating for bruises and restoring circulation. Next to Dirk was a half-finished can of Pabst which cured what little hangover I had. I walked off to find water.

I found out that the couple we had partied with, whom I had taken for bikers, were also scouts for Norton. They were very impressed by me, Dirk said; I had appeared very thoughtful, and they had signed some kind of deal with me for a book-length poem. I never found out what I had signed, but we spent the advance they sent to Marla on one great skydiving and gourmet food weekend at a resort in Tahoe. We were on the road again by noon, and had broken down by six.

What does the open road taste like?

The open road tastes like Winston cigarettes, burned coffee, and salt.

The open road tastes like french fries, Pepsi-Cola, and gasoline still on your hands.

The open road tastes like potato chips, engine oil, antifreeze, beef jerky, taco sauce, ice cream, coolant, and chewing gum.

The open road tastes like country music, ephedrine, dexedrine, and dotted white lines.

It is dawn in Appalachia. There is a van in the mists. There is a Poet beside the van. Steam rises from an arc of golden urine. Near the smoldering ruins of the fire is an apple core. A deer moves away from the apple core and into the underbrush. There is the rustle of cellophane and the flicking of a lighter. There is a sharp inhaling sound and there is a pause, and then a rushing exhalation and a sigh.

And then there will be coffee.

When the *Anthology* won the National Book Award, it was no big deal for us really.

The Whitney did give us a certain satisfaction, admittedly.

Of course, the Lannan was great, not that we needed the money, but it felt good.

When the MacArthur people finally came through, and declared our writing group one collective genius, we were dimly aware that we had made it, but we were preoccupied at that time with the production of the Unknown movie.

And Dirk made a good poet laureate, I have to say.

And, needless to say, we would never turn down another Pulitzer.

We barely had time to squeeze in the ceremony for the Nobel Prize, but the banquet was really quite good.

We got drunk with the Aer Lingus people. We tried to explain to them that we weren't Irish, but they took it with a laugh, saying that we clearly were the heirs of Joyce. I wasn't sure I agreed, but I drowned my skepticism in Guinness.

They gave us some recognition in France: it was the Prix-de-something or the Couer-de-something. Rod Coover gave us some obscure Beaujolais Nouveau.

We felt bad about that Academy of American Poets prize that was supposed to be for an unpublished writer. We got around the requirements by publishing exclusively in pixels of light. Which was not, at the time, considered publishing.

I may have been the only one of us who felt that I was unpublished. Given what I consider publishing to be. A conception, I confess, intrinsically tied to pulp and ink. I confess.

The Linux people gave us a cool award for our "open-source" novel: we got a giant stuffed penguin. Linus Torvald presented it, and then took us out drinking. He insisted on only drinking in establishments where he knew how to "program" free beer, but, despite all the walking, we enjoyed it.

Bill Gates bought us a round of icewater and tried to convince us that he was just like us. That was nice.

There's nothing like the Guggenheim.

And the Booker Prize was a true surprise, we didn't see that one coming.

Frankly, I could take or leave the Oscar (Best Supporting Author), but it does make a classy paperweight.

But we weren't sure what to make of the Newberry and the Caldecott. We thought maybe that was some kind of joke.

On our way west to Kansas, we camped at Alley Springs in the Missouri Ozarks. Frank had flown out to meet us, to meet Gaddis, and to attend our reading at Big Sleep Books. After the reading, some art majors from Washington U. presented us with, by way of a parting gift, a bottle of Moet Chandon White Star, an original oil painting, and about 35 whippets of industrial-grade nitrous oxide. On our way out of town, we managed to get a case of champagne flutes, 99 red balloons, a whippet dispenser, a pack of hot dogs, a bag of marshmallows, a bag of ice, a case of beer (we wanted Budweiser just to immerse ourselves in Saint Louis culture, but Frank reminded us of their deplorable labor practices, so we bought Grolsch instead), and a first aid kit. William and I had the tents pitched by dark, and Dirk started a fire while Frank gathered wood. Pretty soon William was playing ukulele and we were roasting wieners. It was good, we were happy. Dirk opened the Moet Chandon. It was warm, and the cork flew on a gushing spume of sparkling champagne, the pop echoing against the mountainsides. We cheered, toasted Saint Louis, and had a fine meal. Then we brought out the whippets and started filling balloons until the metal dispenser was so cold from the supercooled gas that it threatened to stick to our hands.

Things started to go in and come out. We inhaled gas and commented to each other in strange low voices, like tapes played at half-speed. We laughed and laughed at the same things, at different things, at nothing. There was darkness and I realized I was looking down upon myself from a great distance. Then a point in the darkness began to open into a wild echoing undulating noise. There was a prick of light and warmth that was approaching me. Then the sound became crickets and cicadas and the crackling of fire. The circle of light engulfed me and became the world. I was lying on my back on the picnic table beside an overturned beer. I could hear Frank mumbling about stages of consciousness. Someone released a balloon and it shot off into the night with a flatulent exhalation. As a trickle of sensation began to irrigate my nervous system, I became aware of another presence.

I turned my head slowly away from the fire. A gigantic, shambling monster of insane proportions beside the car, the bag of marshmallows in its teeth, was rummaging around in the trunk. I heard the clanking of the box of metal canisters. The bear put another handful of food into its mouth. There was a piercing squeal of escaping gas and the bear turned to stone.

And swayed. And fell over backwards.

Frank was still talking about stages of consciousness. William and Dirk were prone and motionless. The bear lay there and shuddered and released a slow moan. It had eaten a canister of laughing gas and passed out. It would come to very soon. When it did, it might try to eat us, and we were in no shape to fend off a bear. We had no weapons, probably not even a jack in the trunk. I sat up and looked around desperately. I grabbed the case of beer and the Swiss Army knife. I crawled over to the bear. It smelled like a wet carpet, on its back, eyes vacant, mouth open. With the Swiss Army knife's bottle opener, I cracked a beer and poured it into the bear's mouth. And then another. And then another. And then I dropped another whippet into the dispenser, screwed it shut, filled a balloon, and released the gas into the bear's face.

William staggered to his feet and was stumbling to the underbrush when he saw me sitting there, smoking a cigarette, feeding drugs and alcohol to an inert bear. William and I looked at each other for a few seconds, and then William shook his head slowly, walked into the woods and threw up.

¹ And "Dirk" went to the top of a nameless hill and said to no one in particular: "Behold these signs, given to me. Read them in remembrance of me."

² The Prairie Dog Reserve informational plaque near Devil's Tower said: "Prairie dogs enter the world surrounded by fangs…from the air sudden talons."

³ At one time, 25 billion prairie dogs inhabited the vast middle of the United States; now their numbers have diminished to the point that they have been designated "endangered." The powers responsible for determining that the prairie dog is endangered have decided to remedy this by granting the species their protection. The same powers granting their protection are largely responsible for the prairie dog's problems.

⁴ Beware your enemy's remedies.

⁵ But "Dirk," you ask, how shall I know my enemy?

⁶ Search your unhappiness.

⁷ And the billboard advertised the "Humbird Walk-in Cheese Room."

⁸ And, lo, "Dirk" bypassed the Humbird exit, all the while imagining a humidor for cheese, rows and rows of tubes of string cheese, laid out, eager for lips and flame.

⁹ And "Dirk" saw llamas in Minnesota.

¹⁰ And signs indicating that the Llama Owners of S.E. Minnesota were responsible for two miles of highway in that state's "Adopt-a-Highway" litter clean-up program. Owners. Not "ranchers," or "breeders"—owners.

¹¹ This struck "Dirk" as strange.

¹² Were there, then, competing Llama Owner associations in S.W. Minnesota? in N.W. Minnesota? in N.E. Minnesota? in Central Minnesota? "Dirk" imagined ongoing gang warfare between the rival Llama Owners, each group maneuvering

their herds of llamas onto great open fields where the llamas would then proceed to spit upon their enemies. The oceans of phlegm and mucous. The cries of the wounded. The expectorant epics recited by wandering, spit-blinded bards lauding the speed, trajectory, and pungency of the saliva of legendary llamas. The overwhelming smell.

[13] "Dirk" composed a short poem while driving, or rather remembered a previously composed short poem that had lacked an effective title. "Dirk" now provided the missing title.

[14] "Portion of an Adjectival Definition Arranged Mimetically"

> seven
>
> teen syl
>
> lable...

[15] "Good Food" the cafe reader board declares...isn't that, or rather, shouldn't that be a given? Since a restaurant would never advertise that it served "Mediocre Food," there seems to be a slight case of special pleading inherent in reassurances that an eating establishment serves food that is good to eat: "It's good food...really! Ya gotta believe me!! Really, really good!"

[16] And "Dirk" encountered again a sign he had seen before: the name of a hair parlor: "Curl Up and Dye."

[17] And "Dirk" wondered: Aside from the obvious "cleverness," is there anything to recommend this as a name for a business that is presumably trying to attract customers by appealing to their vanity, their desire to remain young forever? Does such a name invite confidence in the skill of the personnel wielding sharp instruments and chemical poisons? Is that enough to

overcome our innate revulsion with our own mortality?

[18] "Dirk" wondered.

[19] Then scratched his groin absentmindedly as if watching a wasp circle a blade of grass.

[20] And "Dirk" watched a movie entitled *fast, cheap, and out of control*.

[21] And the title resonated with "Dirk" and he wrote it down.

[22] And during his travels "Dirk" passed by many motels and one motel reader board proclaimed: "Recommended by Owner."

[23] And "Dirk" was about to belittle this sign, assigning it a position in his taxonomy next to "Good Food," yes, "Dirk" was about to employ heavy sarcasm while conceding that there was an element of genuine tongue-in-cheek wit, but then the inescapable irony took the form of an anvil and landed on his unshod toes: What could possibly be more permeated with the "Recommended by Owner" ethic than this hypertext *The Unknown*, where every page and every link eventually circles around to the implicit and otherwise recommendation that you support those three crazy lads by buying their book.

[24] "Dirk" grimaced.

[25] "His mark is worse than his might," he said with exaggerated mystery.

[26] And "Dirk" couldn't decide if poetry was 1) always personal, 2) inevitably personal, or, 3) both or neither.

[27] And "Dirk" passed over "Lmuma Creek" on the way to Yakima and a disc golf course which would disappoint him greatly and cause a great gnashing of teeth, as well as assorted imagined blows about the head and shoulders of those responsible. Everyone responsible. Every last one. And then one more.

[28] As a warning.

[29] Punctuation.

³⁰ The horoscope for Capricorn, 20 July 1998, includes the following: "Invention relates to your recipe."

³¹ Colonize the world with koans. Koanize the world with colons.

³² Celestial economics observes the following axiom: We never earn anything, but that doesn't mean we don't deserve everything we get.

³³ Or that we don't deserve more than we earn, anyway.

³⁴ So much surplus and still the insistence on the moral obligation to work. Why the conspiracy against leisure?

³⁵ From whom all blessings flow.

³⁶ And while in Oregon, "Dirk" pondered the mystery that the state forbids motorists to dispense gasoline. Every Oregon gas station is a full-service, and nothing but full-service, enterprise.

³⁷ Every time the station attendants cheerfully approached his car, "Dirk" inwardly recoiled, as if he had landed in the middle of a bad *Twilight Zone* episode about "The Gas Station That Time Forgot."

³⁸ And what explains this continued need for station attendants in Oregon? An incredibly powerful gas station attendant union? An unusually clumsy and/or careless general populace? Creeping Socialism?

⁴⁰ On the way to Crater Lake, "Dirk" passes a financial institution that goes by the name, "Valley of the Rogue Bank."

⁴¹ Quibbles about redundancy aside, at least they have the guts to admit it.

⁴²   theconspiracyas
        yet untitled
        fallen

⁴³ Also, near Oregon, but before Crater Lake, "Dirk" watches a water-skier glide across a desert-smooth lake, an immense

nuclear plant cooling tower looming behind him. An apocalyptic pastoral.

[44] Everything we forget.

[45] And "Dirk" added lines of poetry from one of his friends to the Book of Signs:

> and though the years of crossing
> have marred their clarity
> like stones carried home to retell
> a day at the ocean
>
> I was right
> that the story was waiting
> for loss and obscurity, and beauty
> spent recklessly
> so it could finish
> being told

[46] In San Francisco, "Dirk" strolls across the Golden Gate Bridge with the author of the above lines. Along the way are several emergency call boxes adorned with signs stating:

[47] Emergency Phone and Crisis Counseling

[48] Only in San Francisco, "Dirk's" friend comments.

[49] Yes, "Dirk" thought, and how sad that "only" is an invitation for mockery.

[50] "Dirk" encounters the phrase "methodical visionary" and wants to apply it to himself but realizes that the honor should be William's instead.

[51] And the motto/slogan/name for the 107th Merced County Fair in 1998 was: "Poultry in Motion."

[52] As the entire interstate highway system had apparently

deteriorated all at once, not unlike Oliver Wendell Holmes' "Wonderful One-Hoss Shay," "Dirk" was delayed by innumerable construction projects. Near one, the sign: OPEN TRENCH.

[53] Behold, says Lao-Tzu, the Tao is an unopened trench.

[54] How deep is an unopened trench? asks the Zen Master.

[55] My! How trenchant you are with a penchant for non sequitur.

[56] The better to appropriate your corporeal being, my dear.

[57] Colorado. Interstate 70. Some time in July. 1998. Food Hospital Next Right

[58] I'm sorry, Mrs. M—, your veal calf didn't make it. You'll just have to eat him, I'm afraid. There, there. You knew it was only a matter of time…

[59] At times, "Dirk" felt like the small fog waiting at the mouth of a chilled, freshly opened bottle of beer.

[60] Thus ends the Book of Signs.

And it was so.

The tragic weakness of fiction is that it's too real for itself. Frankness is in our being, not our doing, not our having. Pretend otherwise at your leisure but also at your risk. The Lord created the earth in seven days, and it doesn't even take that to recreate it if you're paying attention. And if you're not? The phone will be disconnected. The consciousness that surrounds you will disconnect you from you. In the smallness of the surrounding life a million small implosions will bring collapsing inward the imagination that once filled limitless space with wailing for a mother's teet. Imagine forever and exist in it and you will find power. I offer you across great distance a hand—a way out from your own self-denial—access to the "that which" you have lived your life running from. Come, my friend. Reach for it.

It is the way for you to become known.

He is not shaking yet, not yet.

He untwists the piece of paper—a page torn from *Cain's Book*—and empties the yellowish powder into the spoon on the glass hotel coffeetable. The TV is on and William is out with Dirk, they went to eat or to do something equally revolting.

With not-yet-shaking hands, Scott manages the candle, and the match, and the candle is lit. He prepares the syringe first, with the rolling paper folded tight around the needle to seal the fit between the needle and eyedropper. And then he holds the spoon over the flame until the powder melts and bubbles. Then with his third hand he holds the spoon while with his other two hands he draws the bubbling liquid into the syringe. Then he holds the works down carefully so carefully, not shaking, and with his fourth and fifth arms takes off his belt. He may be shaking, by now, but only slightly.

He is thinking about Marla. And God.

Scott was hunting everywhere for genius, he was looking for it in the detritus of the street, overturning cans of rubbish in England, asking strangers. It turned out to work as a come-on line with a few foreigners, but why not: Do you have genius? The conversation could splinter in any number of directions after that and he'd come away looking as if he knew something. After all, he had his work to draw on. Not that they noticed, not that they understood. But still.

Genius didn't really make itself clear. It was never apparent. It was a kind of crown some wore and others envied. Or didn't much consider or didn't much care about. It depended, of course, on their DNA, the sperm and the egg that made them. Genius, small and precarious, was only what it was. An infinitesimal speck in the cosmos, compared to the infinite weight of everything that surrounded it, breathing and dead. You could say it was almost not, all be told, that it was not there nor should it ever be. Of this he was entirely unsure. And it was time he killed by thinking this, time which would not return again. It all dissolves into poetry, in the end, he thought, it is all sentence fragments and head-pictures and scents of things now gone, which can soothe a rotting brain. Yes, the brain has line breaks and caesuras. Things which drift off and stop, things which achieve more clarity, things which forever disappear from every horizon. Memory, he thought, is the only genius that matters. Every hour we are drifting into it.

So, in the end, it did not really matter. He had no business looking for genius, it was a thing he would not find. It was the invisible world on a blade of grass, smaller. It was dust motes circling Mount Everest. It was some quality not-quality, who knew? The size of the universe is something we cannot grasp. Scott said this on more than one occasion. An answer is no more no less than itself. It slides into nothingness after it has been spoken. That might be genius. That might be, in which case everything is coated with invisible tracings, and everything is as de Selby postulated.

On the airplane to France I listened to a man talk. He was a tall stooped man with wet-looking gray hair that spiraled in tight natural curls past his ears. His face was pleasant. He had broad lips and clean-shaven unwrinkled tan cheeks. On my way to the toilet he looked at me; his eyes were remote and kind and blue. When he talked his neck was bent forward and his fuzzy eyebrows furrowed over the straight top rim of his glasses.

I maintain a high interest in capitalism because it is vibrant and that has been specifically proven…

His voice came in and out of my ears.

…relevant and the points you made particularly…modus operandi to reconstruct…and the understanding and visualization of the, of the, of the thought and how does it expose itself to, but how does it ah, ah, ah relate to, uhm, ah, other European literature…

His subject was never clear to me; but I imagined him as somebody who thought important ideas, at least at first. He seemed, somehow, a lonely man, and I wondered what he would do in Paris. I wasn't sure if I should feel glad or sad for the passenger he spoke to. The hangover I was recovering from, was trying to sleep off, kept me increasing my desire to intercede. Because I really, in some simple way, wished to gain more insight into his mind. His words were so peculiar.

Well no not presently. I pretty much have to isolate so many things to my world and the world about me at the present time… a general focus, my particular life has had an extremely broad spectrum of interests…

It was, how do you say, a kind of inelegant prose, the constituent parts of which, I thought, formed a poetry. Something I was sure William would understand.

There's a breakdown in the understanding of contemporarism...

Indeed, it occurred to me he might be famous. It was as if, in what I didn't hear, the subject of apocalyptic fears, millennial violence, and political discord rested. But he never quite explained what he thought about these things, or I never did quite hear his explanation, my sleeping pills may have worked too quickly, I may have been away from my mind.

We have certain language terms that are effective...sometimes I use two words in explanation of something....Example, referring to last night, when I asked a couple of questions they were unknowledgeable and they could not express sensibly an answer to any question. They were totally devoid of information on the subject...

When we disembarked I felt much better and thought to look for the gentleman in Customs or else at the luggage wheel, but he was nowhere.

I'm sitting in my room, my computer's humming, and I'm looking at this picture my mom gave me of these cows and men walking through a lake in France. So what happens? The doorbell rings, it's the FedEx guy, and he hands me a little package that I open (not before taking a sip of my beer) to find an airplane ticket to Paris. It's business class, but so what. This is the kind of luck a guy like me has: just when I'm about to sit down at my computer to write a real book, not a goddamn short story, somebody hand-delivers a bottle of whiskey, or I get a call that my literary pack is fucked up in Paris and London, or I get a FedEx with tickets to Paris in it. Fuck all.

Now, the last time I saw Scott and crew, I was thinking and so were they and it was a damn good peyote trip, we were telepathic together. Now they're still on their book tour, which is epic, and they're wasted, just wasted. They've got readings everywhere, at Shakespeare & Co., at Left Bank Books, in Berlin outside the train station, on the train. These are major events and my buds are too drunk to deal. So I figure, cool, a chance to promote my collections of short stories and miscellania—*100 Words 100 Ways*, *The Language of Cereal Boxes: Short Stories from Your Supermarket Shelves*, and *The Fortune Cookie Guide to Living*. The guys are sleeping in the train on the way to Berlin while I conduct their trainboard reading to an audience of French and Germans and international travelers. There I am, reading things like, "You will soon have good luck" (excerpt from *The Fortune Cookie Guide to Living*) and everybody's applauding. It helps that I'm dressed like Scott and they think I'm him—helps in more ways than one (so what if it's my name on the book; I just cross it out and write his in if they ask). People buy me drinks, ladies say to me "Parlez-vous français?" (I say back, you're sweet too). That's how it goes I guess, being a literary American. You're kind of famous. Not big famous, but there's ten people at your friend's reading and they don't care if you read, as long as you answer to his name.

We get through the tour dates in this way and I take the boys to the Swiss Alps: good air, clean living, and women who speak four or five languages that I don't understand. There's a chalet I know about, more like an abandoned building in Bern, where I take my friends. Of course, other people live there, and they happened to be having a party when we arrive. The room is filled, knee deep, in leaves. Jazz plays, Bill Evans. The only lights are candles on candelabra attached to the walls. A pretty girl with red hair stands alone in the corner. Dirk, William, and Scott sort of revive a little for the party, end up talking to some of the various guests about nonsense. They were expecting beds, but end up passing out in piles of leaves and seem happy enough with it. I walk over to the redhead. Turns out she's American, from somewhere around Los Angeles.

We talk about writing. Why do you care to do it, she asks me, it seems silly to write, there are so many books already, so much that's been said. I'd rather do something really well, help people learn something. I don't want my name all over. Why do you like it? I don't know, I say. Perhaps because it helps me chew the hugeness of the subject: what do I know? That's what I'm in it for, I want to know things. I don't speak all that well, I don't think all that well, except sometimes when I write something. Mostly I want to be left alone. Too much has been written, I continue, there's tons of books, but still. Some of the things I've read meant things to me, big things, they helped me feel I wasn't alone in particular, localized, inimitable ways. I want to do that for someone. And I can't not do it, I say, or I think I can't not—I don't want to necessarily, but, again, it's how I think. She says, What do you mean they helped you? Wouldn't something else have helped you? Do you see yourself as some kind of savior? No, I say. I feel bewildered, I say. She's looking at me, I have a half-smile on my face and I realize this is it, this is it. I don't know what it is. I say I don't know what it is because I don't know, or I know, but what do I know? In any case we kiss, or I lean over to kiss her but she turns just at the last minute and I kiss her cheek. She brings her hand up and caresses my head. I don't know what happens.

The next morning we all wake up groggy and alone and it's quiet, except the redhead's still sleeping next to me. I still don't know her name. I buy some chocolate cake and milk and a couple of loaves of good heavy bread and some fruit and we all play Scrabble, me, her, Dirk, and Scott. William sleeps through it, sleeps for twenty-six straight hours, by my reckoning. During the game, there's some debate whether French and German words count (we are, after all, on the Continent), but I point out it was an American-bought game and we play by the rules of English. The redhead wins on the strength of "quim" and "∞" and "zapateo." Dirk tries to recruit her into his cult but she gets annoyed and sticks her tongue out at him; he falls immediately to sleep. Scott takes a walk and falls asleep in a park. I won't tell you what I do. But the next day, everybody's dry. Really, truly. That doesn't happen much. Can I go home now, I say to the guys? Please?

You don't know books unless you know Powell's, okay, that's not the slogan, but whatever. That's something my English teacher in high school used to tell me when he'd get me high in the teacher's lounge. All the English teachers were stoners in that high school—what do you want, I learned from potheads, at least they knew books.

So anyway when things get stressful at home I hop on an airplane and head North. That's what I do. I go to Portland and eat some three buck Spicy Mac and Cheese at Bistro Montage and I drink Rainer pounders and then I shoot pool with the staff until Powell's opens at like nine in the morning, I don't know what time the place opens, who cares.

This was a special occasion anyway, Dirk and Scott and William were there. They didn't tell anybody. This was a stealth reading. I knew because I'm Frank. People need to realize that about me. I know because I'm Frank.

Yeah, okay, strike that last line. I was just saying that. I thought maybe it would mean something but it doesn't. That's a problem, isn't it. Here's my character, let me draw myself: sort of not as tall as William, who's taller than me. Sort of not as balding as Scott, he's got more forehead than me and it burns easily. Sort of not as charismatic as Dirk, that guy leads cults. What do you want? My eyes are bloodshot, even my therapist says so. Nosehairs stick out of my nose. I've got armpit rash and I'm always itching them. When I walk, it's a kind of shuffle. My beard is what you might call full, if I had one, and I don't, but in its place I've got a ton of nicks and cuts and Band-Aids.

That's an overstatement about the nicks and cuts. That's hyperbole. That's exaggeration. My skin is fine like a bottom.

That's bullshit too. I can't help it. Hold up a mirror. What do you see? What do you see in your mirror?

Okay back to the story: it was to be a stealth reading. I don't know if they'd been to Portland or not, who cares. They were back or they were there for the first time and I've got connections. I know a guy who owns dogs. I know a Student Union and I know for a fact it's got couches and I know for a double fact it's okay if they slept there, say if they spent all their money on wine or whatever they spend all their money on. I know other people too: I know a guy who lives in a house and a guy who owns a house and women I know some women and I know a woman who owns a house and I know an old lady. Why'd they want me at this stealth reading? I know them, who knows. Portland's a real pretty city. Do you want me to ramble or tell what happened?

What happened is this. We took acid. We took mushrooms. We took a whatever, it was stuff in somebody's bag, we didn't care. It was warm. Real warm. We parked someplace in Sellwood and hiked down the railroad tracks and picked bunches of blackberries and put them in huge containers and set some little sticks we had on fire and drank beer and ate berries and extemporized. William has the transcripts, he took copious notes.

A train rolled by and that interrupted things and it got dark slowly in increments that lasted forever. Somebody took out a ukulele, maybe this was William, he stopped taking notes and played songs. People joined us, a bunch of hipsters from Reed College, they had nice voices and sang songs and then disappeared, maybe they went to a party. Giant animals came and cuddled with each of us, we went off in separate directions, another train passed and stopped, it parked in our driveway and a mariachi band disembarked, played for us *canciones de Mexico*, handed us fortune cookies, then rode off in their train. The blackberries did a dance. The darkness split up into pieces, fragmented entirely. We fell asleep like dominoes and every one of us was double five.

We woke up and the sun was way up in the sky high up. We were late for the reading. The reading wasn't at Powell's, I hope you didn't think it was. Powell's is just this great huge bookstore and we spent three or four hundred dollars each there, either before or after the reading, I don't remember. Just say we browsed for hours and bought like were starving and left with bags too heavy to carry, we had to hire porters.

This actually was why the reading was a stealth reading. We needed a tax write-off to get to Powell's and buy books. It's not sexy, it's not hip. But that's the way it was. We had a solid reason to be there, we went, we bought books. All this only need be mentioned. You don't need to see it happening. The stacks are high at Powell's. If you were to see us there, it might bore you. We stood and thumbed through new books. We stood and thumbed through old books. We smelled books. We drank coffee. We went from the purple room to the blue room to the pink room. That's what we did. It lasted forever, I can't remember if it happened earlier or later in this narrative, it doesn't matter I tell you.

Now about the reading. That's why we're here, fictionally and otherwise. There was a reading. It took place about three on a sweaty day. The day wasn't sweating, we were. Roses were in bloom not far from us. We were under the Burnside Bridge. A bunch of punks were skateboarding. We didn't have an audience at the start. The Columbia flowed behind us, its salmon dying.

Dirk took the stage first. He read silently, without moving his lips, for about forty minutes. It was beautiful.

Scott read next. He played an air guitar and not so much read as recited Kafka's "Letter to His Father." I don't know why he picked that one. His eyes were closed the whole time. The sounds of the skateboarders began to slow at some point during his recitation.

I took the stage next. I did hopscotch routines I'd been working on. This wasn't poetry, this wasn't fiction. Or was it? I thought of it as mood movement. As I hopscotched I sang a poem I'd created in the shower one afternoon in San Francisco. It was a short song, a line or two, I can't remember what it was now. But people clapped when I ended. There was a breeze.

William took the stage next. When I say stage, I don't mean stage, I mean concrete. This wasn't a stage. Somebody handed me a cigarette, which I didn't want. I took a Lemon Drop from my pocket instead. William read. He read a long poem he'd written backwards. Then he read it side to side. Then he read it upside down. All the skateboarders by now were clapping in rhythm to his poem. When he started to read the poem upside down, William began doing a strange dance. He'd shuffle three steps to his left, then shuffle three steps to his right. Then he'd do it again. Then he'd throw his arms in the air and look up, as if searching for God in a bridge. Then he'd shuffle three steps forwards and then he'd shuffle three steps backwards. Then he'd throw his arms to the ground, as if coaxing a mint plant to sprout. All this time he'd read his poem upside down.

Not a lot of people know about this reading. It was a secret reading. When it concluded, we drove out to a BBQ joint I know on 82nd Street and ate chicken, hot and spicy, then we went to Bagby Hot Springs to soak in the water and come clean.

We get off Amtrak at Davis and steal some bikes. They were sitting there, unchained, some college kids' bicycles. Scott starts riding no-handed and crashes once; William begins singing an aria, but really it's a passage from Schopenhauer, I don't know which one, he's singing it in Spanish for some reason. Dirk takes off his shirt and makes fart noises as he rides. The craziness, surely, has something to do with the whiskey we drank on the train. I kept winning at cards so I didn't drink, but the others, well, you know the story. It doesn't have to be told.

We're headed to Freeborn Hall for a KDVS radio special. But it occurs to me, as we maneuver though groups of students, men wearing shirts advertising their fraternities and women in skirts and others in shorts and so on and so forth (imagine a college town and the easy streets with young people walking down it, going in and out of shoe stores and record stores and bookstores and drugstores; imagine a flat college town, one that's hot where everybody wears shorts in the summer and women wear these shirts that show off their midriffs to enticing effect, imagine the buildings and the classes and the student union and the people trying to give away credit cards and the people trying to get signatures to free political prisoners in African and Latin American and Asian and European and North American countries and imagine all the rest, the hippies sitting in a circle passing a joint and the guys on the basketball court shooting hoop and a lone woman under an oak tree reading *Crime and Punishment* and a couple walking toward the library and and and).

We reach Freeborn Hall for our interview. But a curious thing has happened. Dirk, it appears, proving de Selby's theory about bicycles, or at least giving it some degree of credence, can't dismount. It appears for a moment that he has become part bicycle. This gives some degree of satisfaction. On the train, I'd been explaining de Selby's theory that bicycle thieves often turn into the bicycle they've stolen. But no one had listened. (They hadn't disagreed; merely, they hadn't listened.) I couldn't remember the whole theory; I only knew a part of it. However, I did remember de Selby's strange remedy: hit the seat with your hand. Bicycles don't like to be hit on their seat, it bugs them. Dirk hits the seat. The bicycle slowly, reluctantly let him go.

You can imagine the rest.

He began wishing there were some way to record everything he spoke, such were the pearls of wisdom that regularly dropped from his swinish lips. This was not a unique idea; he remembers encountering it in superhero comic books: usually, the villain, the Fantastic Four's nemesis, Dr. Doom, for example, keeps a running record of everything he says and does: a perpetual home video. Aspiring to match the egotism of a comic book super-villain gives him pause. He realizes he is probably experiencing something akin to the error of those practitioners of Zen who reach a preliminary level of transcendental awareness, a level that convinces them that they are completely enlightened, though, in truth, they have simply run into another illusion to discard. Apparently, this delusion of godhood undoes some; others survive it and continue on the path to enlightenment. Still, the appeal of saving all his words was difficult to discard, until it occurred to him that to do so would be to admit poverty. Surely, his fecund brain would always generate a surplus; he should be generous with his pronouncements, let them fall where they may, like the like the poems Li Po wrote on maple leaves, then delivered to a river.

THE BLAND TASTE

by

D.S. Quelirot

'Ithwæ yma ownay eyesai Iæ awsei erhai ittingsay yba
erhaielſsæ andai enwhæ ethay oysba aidsey ota erhai:
Atwhey odæ ouyay antway?; eshai ouldwei eræsponday:
Iæ ishwey Iæ erewey anai carosæ eyermei einerwey.'

For Marvin Fenda
e pluribus unum

I. The Aerial of the Dead

McDonald's is my kind of place, grilling
Hamburgers out of dead cattle, frying
Grease and blood, toasting
Sesame seed buns.
And while still warm, dressing
With pickles and onions, mixing
Mustard and mayonnaise.
The cops surprised us near First and Main
While we were cruising; we got pulled over
And they gave us a ticket for speeding,   10
So we parked and drank beer and listened for sirens.
Here I sit upon the pooper, shitting out another Trooper.
During the weekend you're your own person,
Styx and stones and erogenous zones,
And the answer my friend is pistons in the wind:
On Friday and Saturday night—then you feel free...
On Monday, school starts again and you have to go back.

Where are your restrooms, your urinals
Your stalls of relief? Son of a bitch,
Why isn't there ever enough toilet paper?   20
You always find an empty roll or one tattered sheet
And you can't use the paper towels
And you can't leave the stall,
You are trapped in the shadows
(Sitting in the shadow of the stall) staring
At your neighbor's feet, relieved but not finished.
            Here I sit
            All Broken-hearted
            Tried to shit
            But only farted.   30
'Last dance he gave me an orchid;
'This time I get a pink carnation.'

'God, my hair's a mess. I wish this night
'Were over. He'll probably try to kiss me.'
When I stare at the revolving mirrored ball,
Gazing in the bitter glass,
These things I know: A hard man is good to find. And
A fart is powerful as a king.

    Madame Psoriasis, famous hairdresser,
(And part-time phrenologist)   40
Has a hangnail, nevertheless is known to be
The wisest woman in the suburbs. Use, said she,
Clorox liquid bleach for the tough stains and
Fluoride toothpaste for fewer cavities.
Put Litter Green in your catbox but have
Air freshener on hand just in case. Dust with Pledge
And buy Odor Eaters for your husband's shoes.
Put a tiger in your tank.
You may squeeze the Wonder Bread but you
Are forbidden to squeeze the Charmin. Watch out for   50
Embarrassing underarm stains. Fear flaking and itching.
Wisk around the collar, don't ring around the collar.
Thank you. If you see dear Mrs. Monotone
Tell her I will be by her home myself:
Bing bong! Avon calling!

    Burger King
Under the orange plastic and neon
Crowds flow through your doors, so many
I had not thought convenience had undone so many.
Whoppers, fries, onion rings, Cokes,   60
Pass quickly over your counters,
Through several digestive tracts,
Once around and then it's back
Being sold again from noon until midnight
Ground dead meat on a toasted bun.

There I saw one I knew and stopped him, crying: 'Sucrose!
'You were with me when we cruised Main!
'Those cows you entombed in andalusian pianos
'Have they crossed the floor as planned?
'You had better starve that Dog of yours   70
'Or he'll eat hamburger between shows
'And make a fool of himself in front of the cameras!
'Don't look up here! The joke's in your hand!'

II. A Chain of Regress

    The Ham sat upon a silver platter
Centerpiece of the polished table,
Ringed by pineapple slices and glazed with brown
Sugar. Near the Ham a lone candlestick
Sputtered lazy, smoky threads ceiling-ward
And beyond. The peas wrinkled greenly
In their own baroque bowl of sterling   80
Munificence. Caesar salad wilted
Untouched on expensive china; egg,
Vinegar and oil swimming separate
Paths to identical destinations.
The soup cools and thickens in its serving
Bowl shading a plate of carvéd pommes des terre.
The wine, at the head of the table, sits,
Unopened, ignored—but still a very good year.
Beneath this spacious feast the host and hostess
Answer nature's creative primal   90
Urge with missionary zeal. No guests
Will stumble upon this sybaritic scene
And hear the grunts and moans: violent
Noise that fills all, even the dessert.
And still she cries—'Unh! Unnnnh!' forgetting
The withered stumps of other times.
Replacing the shackles of parental
Admonishment with the joy
Of spontaneity they copulate
As barnyard animals amidst the straw,   100
A final heave, and premature grunting
Spills into gasps, ravaged and still.

    What's the matter with Bill tonight?
    He seems to be on edge.
'It's caffeine. Caffeine makes him irritable.

'The doctor told him not to drink coffee.'

Have you tried Sanka brand?

'Decaffeinated coffee has no taste.'

Not Sanka brand.

Sanka has a full rich flavor. 110

The fine flavor of Colombian, mountain-grown beans.

'Really? We'll try some today!'

Good

Morning folks! How are Bill's nerves today?

'Great!

'I feel just great!'

'Thanks to Sanka, Bill can fill it to the rim!'

'Sanka brand makes me feel like dancing!'

But

O O O O that disco beat 120

It's so overrated

So constipated

'What do you want to do now?'

'I don't care. What do you want to do?'

'I don't know.'

'Wanna play some pinball?'

The throbbing bells

And lights respond when play is hot.

And if you miss the special

Or three times drain away, just put another quarter in the slot. 130

When he finally dumped her, I said,

Well, it's about time, I told her,

GO FIGHT WIN TONIGHT

In fact, I think you should have dumped him

I said, he was only after your body you know.

But she wouldn't listen to me and was talking

About letting him do it! Can you believe that?

And she'll probably 'forget' to protect herself

And her with her irregular period

And everything. She says she's in love 140
But I think she's just being stupid.
GO FIGHT WIN TONIGHT
Well if she gets herself pregnant
She can't say she wasn't warned!
She'll only have herself to blame.
GO FIGHT WIN TONIGHT
GO FIGHT WIN TONIGHT
And just you watch, he'll leave her again anyway.
Well, ba-bye. I'm going over to see Albert. Ba-bye.
Ba-bye, ba-bye. 150
Ba-bye Mary, ba-bye Kathy, ba-bye, ba-bye.

III. The Tire's Turn On

The flag pole rope is broken: the metal clasps rattle
Against the pole, pushed by the flatulent wind
Crossing the asphalt. The customers are departed.
So get up and get away...
The parking lot bears no Styrofoam burger boxes,
Straws, napkins, paper bags, beer cans
Or other testimony of teenage gluttony. The customers are departed.
And their friends, the ones wearing trainee caps
Have departed after sweeping the grounds.   160
'You, you're the one! You deserve a break today,
'You, you're the one! So come in and have it your way.'
But in the back of my mind I feel
Satanic transformations of the supper meal.
A white rat crept softly through the maze
Protruding pink eyes following a nose
Around endless antiseptic corners
For one more piece of cheese. In a Skinner Box
One need not think except about which levers
Should be pressed with your rat's foot   170
To stop the shock or win the prize.
But, again, in the back of my mind I feel
Someone has prompted the contestants, made a deal,
Like flashers they have secrets hidden beneath their coats:
'I can name that tune in zero notes.'
Do I want the box or Door Number Three...
Five rolls of toilet tissue, life-time guarantee!
And one hundred trips to a dime stall free!
Don't throw toothpicks in the urinals!

Kiss kiss kiss   180
Hug hug hug hug hug hug
So rudely french'd
By you

McDonald's
Awash in the neon of a midnight noon
'He asked me to go to a drive-in
'With him next Saturday night.'
'Gawd, how gross!
'You aren't going to go are you?'
'I couldn't say no. He looked so desperate.   190
'Besides, I want to see the movies.'

    I Tiremichelin, though portly, throbbing between
Two languages, watch the action at the drive-in,
Where, behind the wheels of jacked-up cars
The young try to meet an older version of themselves
Beneath the nudity of their innocence.
I Tiremichelin, androgynous white hulk, of soft
And tired body, perceive these scenes
Yet still I cannot tell you what it means.
During these twilight hours, when lovers strive   200
Upward and inward, clothes removed and askew
Legs perilously spread, passions in overdrive
Amid frantic whispers of 'I love you!'
During the second feature he makes his move
Motivated by his lust and the need
To join the locker room ranks, to prove,
He too, can find some action, spill his seed.
His hurried kisses go unprotested,
But he is unable to undo her bra
Leaving her breasts safe and unmolested,   210
His virgin fingers frustrated and raw.
Desperately he tries to unzip her pants;
This last assault she pushes aside
With sharp words and a withering glance;
His ardor begins to quickly subside.
And when finally the movie ends
He knows exactly what to tell his friends:

'If they ask me how far I got to go
'I'll smile and say, "Do I look like a sap?
'"Is the Pope Catholic? Does the wind blow?
'"I don't just leave popcorn in a girl's lap!"'   220
Meanwhile his date wishes time moved faster.
'I should have known, I should have known,' she thought,
'A date with him would be a disaster.
'And now he'll brag about how far he got.'

    He escorts her to the porch stair
'Go out next Friday?' he asks hopefully
'I'm certain I will be washing my hair,'
She replies, closing the door on his knee.
'Women!' he mutters, as he limps to his car.   230
When will sex be more than a Vaseline jar
A Playboy foldout smuggled home
Locked bedroom doors
Inadmissible Trojans hiding in underwear drawers.

                Armpits sweat
                Oily dirt
                The smell drifts
                Towards watering eyes
                The fumes
                Rise   240
                From a stained heavy cotton shirt
                The victim looks
                For his spray
                Deodorant
                That will last all day
                        Spraylasprayla spray
                        Spraylaspray sprayla spray

                Two young women
                Stroll across

A tennis court   250
Towards boyfriends.
'Give me a Certs
'My breath offends—
'My albatross!'
'Here. Now breathe
'In—taste that fresh
'Breath feeling,
'Candy mint sparkle.'
          Woahooooh woooh
          Woahwoooh ohwahooooo   260

And then once we tried
To do it in a VW Rabbit
The brake slipped and we began to slide
We had to stop to grab it.

And my feet were out the window
We both got cramps in our legs and necks
His arm hit the horn and made it blow—
But, I mean, where else can you have sex?

When I'm high
Like everything   270
Becomes inoperative
Man, and I can fly: I can fly
Like a butterfly and be like a sting
You know?
                    yeh yeh

With Cannabis I turn on

Turning turning turning turning
O wow man I'm so fucked up
O wow man I'm so fucked
turning on   280

IV. Rinse With Water

Phyllis wasn't always so popular you know,
Her hair used to be lifeless, and dandruff-flaked
Stringy and limp.
                    She never had dates.
Spent the weekends alone. Alas, her heart ached.
But then one day things turned around!
Phyllis discovered:
                    Another shampoo!
It made her hair shiny, gave it body and life.
Consider Phyllis, who was once just as ugly as you.   290

V. Lots of Wonder Bread

After the dinner in suit and tie
After the painful silences at the dance
After the clumsy kiss good-bye
The fumbling and the tightening
Of lips and teeth and retraction
Of tongue behind your tonsils
Those were girls between his thighs
You recall them saying frightening
Yourself into impotence

Civilization is soap but there is none   300
No soap just water and the paper towels
The towels rolled on the wall above the sink
Which is a sink with water but no soap
If there were only soap above this sink
Here one could wash and sit and think
There is not even toilet paper in the stalls
But bare wooden rollers with tissue
There is not even graffiti on the walls
But clean painted surfaces that dare
You to deface them   310
                              If there were gas
And acid
If there were gaseous acid
And indigestion
And gas
A pool
An acid pool in a stomach
If there were the sound of belching
Not gurgling
Nor rumbles of hunger   320
But the sound of acid against the lining
Where ulcers burrow in the blood-soft flesh

Plop plop fizz fizz—fizz fizz fizz
Ah, what a relief it spells

How many golden arches are there above
Cracked asphalt parking lots filled
With innumerable automobiles
How many drive-in windows
Are carved into restaurant walls
For the marriage of steel and brick and flesh   330
And how many billions will be served
And eaten
Arby's Wendy's Hardee's
McDonald's Burger
King

A deacon, with some white bread prepares
The Lord's Supper by trimming the crust away
And cutting what's left into tiny squares
Placing them on a tray
Of engraved silver. Unfermented grape   340
Juice will be poured into tiny glasses
A sterile communion for the masses
Who like to eat identical meals in tight and orderly groups.

In the faint moonlight the restaurant
Surrounded by scattered litter:
Lasciate ogn speranza voi eh'entrate!
There are the cash registers, the trash barrels where
Dry buns are discarded.
There is the empty grill
Final resting place of innumerable beeves   350
We have butchered the beeves of the sun
And scattered their hooves on the sea
The smell of dead meat is on our fingers.
Then a fart in darkness. A dry gust of
Carrion comfort.

Lover's Lane was quiet, a full
Moon hid behind black clouds
Those not cruising, are here
Couples lurched and humped in silence.
Then broke the wind   360
BLAH
Video: what do you see?
My brother, tubes taking their minds
The lawful snaring of the potential spender
(With eighteen per cent interest attached)
Buy this, and this also, they insist
The dead are not found only in mortuaries
For memories reshaped by the beneficent networks
Share seats and meals with lean cadavers
In their slumber rooms   370
BLAH
Vichyssoise: I have heard them say
Give to us, give to us this day
Our daily bread and circus
Two all beef patties special sauce
Lettuce cheese pickles onions
On a sesame seed Clown
BLAH
Venery: She responded
But wouldn't move to the back seat   380
I promised her everything, my love, my heart
Hoping to give the beating
To other hands

                              I sat upon the curb
Staring, with the Burger King behind me
Shall I at least change the channel?
Ring around the collar the collar the collar
O che sciagura d'essere senza coglioni
A fabis abstinete—Kilroy was here

For a good time call Phyllis
They wash these walls to stop my pen
But the Shithouse Poet strikes againe!
Video. Vichyssoise. Venery.

       Sanskrit   sanskrit   sanskrit

Notes on the Bland Taste

The plan and a good deal of the incidental episodes of the poem were suggested to me after years of watching television. Indeed, so deeply am I indebted, television will elucidate the fatuities of the poem much better than my notes can do; and though I do not recommend it, it may be that a few months of television will be necessary for any who think such elucidation of the poem worth the trouble. To another institution I am indebted in general; I mean the 'fast food' franchise; I have used especially references to the two largest, McDonald's and Burger King. Anyone who is acquainted with these restaurants will immediately recognize where the title of the poem originates.

I. THE AERIAL OF THE DEAD

Line 12. V. Hardwick Union Building, Men's Bathroom, Stall 3. It should be noted that graffiti locations are extremely unreliable due to the constant efforts of custodians to eliminate it.

14. Styx. V. Milton, *Paradise Lost*, II, 577.

15. Cf. Bob Dylan: "The answer my friend is blowin' in the wind."

20. A phenomenon that I have often noticed.

26. Cf. The job's not finished until the paperwork is done.

27. Cowles Memorial Library, Men's Bathroom, Stall 2.

32. Cf. What would the United States be if everyone owned a pink car?

36. Cf. Yeats, "The Two Trees":
There, through the broken branches, go
The ravens of unresting thought;
Flying, crying, to and fro,
Cruel claw and hungry throat,
Or else they stand and sniff the wind,
And shake their ragged wings; alas!
Thy tender eyes grow all unkind:
Gaze no more in the bitter glass.

37. V. Sea-Tac International Airport, South Concourse, Women's

Bathroom, Stall 16.

38. V. Nikarchos, *Greek Anthology*, II, 395. The whole poem is of great
scatological interest:

If blocked a fart can kill a man

if let escape, a fart can sing

health-giving songs; farts can kill and save:

a fart is powerful as a king.

51. Embarrassing underarm stains. Cf. Part III, 235-247.

Fear flaking and itching. Cf. Part IV, 282.

57. The interior of the Spokane, Washington Burger King on the
corner of Francis and Division is, to my mind, one of the ugliest
and incongruous interiors of any fast food establishment I have
ever seen.

66. $C_{12}H_{22}O_{11}$.

68. Cf. *Un chien andalou*. I have obviously departed from the film for
my own convenience.

73. V. San Francisco, California, Ansonia Residence Club, Second
Floor Bathroom.

II. A Chain of Regress

88. Chateau-Mouton Rothschild, 1966.

91. According to Kinsey, the most widely used sexual position.

98. Cf. Alex Comfort, *The Joy of Sex*.

119. Cf. Leo Sayers.

III. The Tire's Turn On

162. V. Stevens, "Gubbinal."

164. This is *Rattus novegicus* var. *albinus* which I have often seen used for
experimental purposes. Skinner says (in *The Behavior of Organisms*):
"It has the advantage... of submitting to the experimental
control of its drives and routine of living... [and] the rat has the
following added advantages... [i]t is cheap and cheaply kept...."
Its "mindlessness" is justly celebrated.

179. Mead, Washington, Mead Senior High School, Men's
Gymnasium Bathroom, Urinal 3. The graffiti in its entirety

reads: "Don't throw toothpicks in the urinals! The crabs can pole vault!"

192. Tiremichelin, though a mere voyeur and not indeed a 'character' is yet the most important assemblage in the poem absorbing all the rest. Just as McDonald's melts into Burger King, and the latter is not wholly distinct from Wendy's or Hardee's, so all hamburgers are the same hamburger and everything is consumed by Tiremichelin. What Tiremichelin *sees*, however, is just a part of the poem.

207. Cf. Genesis 38.9.

232. Cf. Miss April, 1980. 35-24-34.

234. Cf. *Odyssey*, VIII. Also, *Aeneid*, II.

254. Cf. Coleridge, *The Rime of the Ancient Mariner.*

258. Cf. "It's a candy mint! It's a breath mint!"

264. I.e., the brake lever.

271. Cf. Ron Zeigler: "That statement is now inoperative."

273. Cf. Muhammed Ali, "Float like a butterfly / Sting like a bee."

V. Lots of Wonder Bread

In the first part of Part V three themes are employed: a boy's first kiss, rest room inefficiencies (see Part I, l. 20 and note) and acid indigestion.

300. V. Heinrich von Tritschke.

346. V. *Inferno* iii, 9.

350. Cf. John Crowe Ransom: "murdering of innumerable beeves."

355. V. Gerard Manley Hopkins.

362. Video, vichyssoise, venery. These lines were suggested to me by some graffiti I encountered in Eugene, Oregon: "vidi vici veni," which is, of course, a transposition of Caesar's famous words recorded by Seutonius in *Lives of the Caesars*, sec. 37.

365. Cf. Pound, Canto XLV.

372. Vichyssoise. I had in mind Bon Vivant Vichyssoise, designated by *Esquire Magazine* as the Worst Flavor of the Decade (1970's).

373-74. V. Oakland: "Give to us this day our daily bread / and circus."

388. V. Voltaire, *Candide*.

389. A fabis abstinete. Attributed to Pythagoras by Robert Burton in *Anatomy of Melancholy*.

390. Cf. Variations in rest rooms around the world.

391-92. Vantage, Washington, Shell Station Men's Room.

394. Sanskrit. Repeated as here, an informal prophecy of expected critical response.

Who would have believed that, in the closing days of the twentieth century, humankind's literature was being criticized by an intelligence far greater than its own? While writers scurried to and fro between their readings at universities and visiting professorships and residencies at writers' workshops, their words were being studied as carefully as DNA might be decoded by a geneticist beneath a powerful microscope. Trapped in their earthy plane, and their linear thought, these poets and novelists' lines were as predictable as the behavior of ants. But for a few exceptions. Because a few writers had become freed from that plodding page-turning that begins at i and continues through 1079 that had imprisoned human thought for two millenia, and were producing a text the sheer complexity of which was enough to intrigue the observers, and give them cause to write criticism. But their efforts to radio this useful feedback to the creatures of earth failed, because the four hypertext novelists could barely afford shoes, much less the sophisticated directional electro-magnetic instruments necessary to understand and receive guidance from the criticism. And so this intelligence realized it was necessary to make a trip across the ocean of space that separated it from earth, in order to help the human race evolve into a form of intelligence capable of writing the sort of hypertext novels that this intelligence required to make it laugh.

In space they took Dirk away and they made him write things. Lots of things. He was fed through an umbilical and in a glass sphere he wrote for days without stopping and the aliens observed him.

I remember that time didn't pass while we were in orbit. I could see the earth, and I watched with fascination its storms and seasons. I had never would never again see anything so beautiful. We circled it once every ten minutes. The sun rose and set over a swirling blue horizon. I now fully understood my love for this planet, this sweet bluegreen weedgarden that had grown a literature. Its soft salty oceans, its sandy shores, starfish, seaweed, and languages. The people I loved because I remembered them. I remembered Ed from Phoenix and Marla and my grandmother and my daughter, who would be born in 2010. I remembered my death and my birth as if they happened on the same afternoon. I remembered Barth, Krass-Mueller, Rettberg, as if they were the same memory. I could smell Kansas and I could see the ocean in San Diego. I could feel the heat of Albuquerque and the cold of Manitoba. I could taste the coconut shrimp we ate with Newt Gingrich mingled with the Tucher Hefe-Weizen I drank the night Dirk shot the TV. I could read every page of the anthology and every link of the hypertext was visible at once, forming a rotating four-dimensional model in my mind. I was having an orgasm and sleeping and drinking coffee and finishing my novel *I Will Keep the Home Fires Burning*. It was 2020 and 1969. I was having sex with everyone I ever had or would have sex with at once, while reading the *New York Times* 13 October 1998.

And then I opened my eyes and caught Mark Amerika stealing my cigarettes from beneath my pillow.

After his death, Dirk shed his corporeal form, and floated, like a spirit, only not quite, like a soul, but he didn't believe in that, like a shade, but more the kind you'd sit in under a tree than a ghost, like a, what, like a Jungian archetype, no, like the zeitgeist, that's not it exactly, it is difficult to describe, this thing that Dirk was after he had been so brutally slaughtered, puréed on the altar of circumstance, made a sacrificial offering of, carefully excised from the map of human endeavor, no, that's not it, that's too much to say that, for indeed, if anything, his loss was his gain, as it were, in terms of the popular consciousness, in the way that these things happen to artists after they are dead, as had happened to William Gaddis, whose *A Frolic of His Own* began flying off the shelves soon after his life-force had expired, whose works were suddenly being taught in freshman composition classes the world over, yes, Dirk too, this had happened to, as Oprah had the rest of us on her show to promote the anthology and to discuss the latest Unknown title, *The Teachings of Dirk*, as women wearing black veils were gathering in town squares across this great nation and others to mourn, as old men were seen weeping in their steins of domestic beer, as Clinton, nearly out of office, himself offered words of reconciliation and condolence, as children everywhere, boychild and girlchild, born fresh unto the Earth, were newly baptized "Dirk" and "Dirkina" and "Dirkelle" and "Strat," as an amateur astronomer, working late into the night, gazing at the stars in between line breaks of "The Bland Taste," spotted a new comet in the night sky and assigned it the appellation of "Stratton's Star," so it went, and this was not a small breath of acknowledgement, this was not fifteen minutes of fame, this was hours of it, and it went on, and so it went, and he did not, he would not, fade from it, and his message was spread, and there were many in his tribe as they cried out in early hallucinogen-drenched mornings, "We are Dirk! We is one!" and it was as if the whole thing had been planned, or rather not planned, but a pattern which rose out of the chaos, and children were planting trees in his name, and I am not avoiding here the impossibility of life after death, I am embracing it, for who am I to say, who am I to deny, that Dirk's was a living spirit, and one which traveled, and soared, and sank, through multitudes, in those earliest moments of the twenty-first century, as Dirk was a pilgrim who had finally made it to Mecca, bowing before the great stone at the same time as he was a monk levitating inches in a monastery in Tibet at the same time as he was a banker watching his Internet stocks come crashing down at the same time as he was an electrician working twenty-four hour days for weeks at a time as the grids slowly returned to normal function at the same time as he was an Ethiopian with no shoes running across the cracked and barren earth, dreaming of distance, at the same time as he was a nun momentarily contemplating a man whom she might have loved had she not taken the vow at the same time as he was an angry teenager flipping burgers for a national chain and seeing no future in the world we had made at the same time as he was a note in a song that the whales made as they sang to each other a song of woe for their brothers who had passed, and were dying, in the devastated ocean, as part of Dirk occupied the taste buds on the tongue of a three year-old girl eating an ice-cream sandwich for the first time, and another part of him absorbing the pain of an eighty-five year-old woman as the explosion tore through her home in Kosovo, killing her husband of sixty years as the brick wall came crashing on his side of the bed, Dirk was in her wail, Dirk was in the streets, dancing with the half-naked crowds in Brazil, Dirk was a woman in the south of France who had just invented a new epistemology, who is to say that he was not there, that he was not in all of these people, that he was even in the lemurs in Madagascar, this is what he claimed, this is what he said, this is what he felt and I would be a liar if I said that I looked in his eyes as he told me these things and did not believe that they were true. There were no scars from pounded nails, there was no fingering of the slices in his side, but he said what he said with feeling, he said it once more, with feeling, and I know that what he said was true.

Things got screwy without real sleep. We couldn't tell time from space for awhile. Time was the motion of the car and time stopped when we did. Then things started to move backwards, and then in more than one direction at once. We began each day by finishing the few drops that remained in the bottle that, later that night, we would crack the seal on and open. We didn't know which draft this was.

So what is to be done is what we are discussing. Frank doesn't know, doesn't know, and then stirs his mate as if to draw the matter out. Dirk has had perhaps too much gin and in his eyes there is only jazz and cigarette smoke, and a tear that might form like a drop of the Seine underneath this electric night at the bottom of the world. There is art, and there is politics, muses William, but he has already lost us, and Scott is looking at Marla across the room where she sits on the edge of the couch stroking the cat and he can only think: "If."

Dirk has stood up somewhat unsteadily to put another record on and this time it is Billie Holiday, a bird in a golden cage. William has seen Scott looking at Marla and he is trying to put together this terrible jigsaw puzzle, this child's game, with his numb and yellowed fingertips. For awhile there is the issue of cigarettes and as Frank passes around a pack of Gauloises we are relieved of that terrible uncomfortableness that is all a part of not-knowing. And then there is a silence as we are swept toward the center of the record where everything is named. And then there is the crackle of the needle in its last dance into the end of the spiral and then only Dirk: "Do records spin the other way in the northern hemisphere?"

And we will argue about how to say "Coriolis force" in French but the matter, like so many other edges in this puzzle, cannot be suitably resolved, and we can no longer escape the sense that the end of the night is near.

What fabulous party in which high-rise were you dreaming about, Marla?

You wake up in a hotel room you don't recognize. You are hung over, and still wearing your skirt, lying on top of the covers. As you stumble to the bathroom, loosening your necklace, you check your pockets to make sure you have your keys, wallet, cell phone, and you look for clues. A business card. And you remember: this is the person you were drinking with last night, the person who represents a large organization, the organization that is going to buy *The Unknown*. Finally, taking it and the other Unknown off your hands.

Making you rich? Probably not.

Successful? Probably not.

But finished, forever freed of the Unknown? Yes.

You splash cold water on your face, tear the plastic off a hotel glass, and try to force down an ibuprofen.

You fail.

Marla...

Dirk is working out now.

He is lying on his back on the floor in his apartment, hands in the air. On each hand is a stack of books he is lifting repetitively.

On his left hand are the book-length poems, all hardbound: Pound's *Cantos*, *Ark*, Olson's *Maximus Poems*, Zukofsky's *A*, *Leaves of Grass*, and, at William's suggestion, *Bad History* by Barrett Watten.

On his right hand are the recent postmodern novels, again all hardbound, some signed: *The Big Joke*, *Underworld*, *Mason and Dixon*.

He does thirty lifts, veins bulging on his powerful arms.

Then, clutching the heaviest volumes to his chest, he begins to do a series of abdominal crunches, silently, methodically, eyes straight ahead. After several hundred repetitions, he divides the books into two large, handled canvas bags and executes a series of curls until his biceps threaten to explode from the amount of blood being pumped into their fatigued fibers. Without resting, Dirk then lifts the bags above his head and begins an equally tor-turous set of tricep presses. Next, he began to do reverse curls, his Popeye-sized forearms quivering from the strain.

His expression is inscrutable, though verging on grim.

This is the point at which he decides to stop reading fiction and to stop writing poetry, and to write exclusively in the medium of transgressive cult religions.

And a movement is born.

William, who had, according to all appearances, been just as or even more excited than any of the rest of us about the prospects of seeing our hypertext brought to the big screen as a major studio release, did not, in fact, take well to the atmosphere of Los Angeles. There is a lot of work involved in moving a film from the concept to the can, most of it social work. There are producers to meet, backers to pitch, directors to choose, stars to select and/or woo. The difficulties we encountered as a result of the groundswell of interest in Dirk's cult activities were to be expected, but I had expected better from William. We were all a little apprehensive about moving from a psychic atmosphere described by one critic as "Midwestern Literary Evangelism" and another as "Techno-Pastoral" to one that could only be described as "Bedding Down with Satan." The devil wears a thousand guises in Hollywood, but such are the costs of seeing a dream to its full fruition.

Film was a medium that none of us could even begin to understand, but we knew that it had been the art form of the twentieth century. While we have our understanding of collaboration, in Tinsel Town, collaboration takes on an altogether different pallor; it is the stuff of bitter feuds and power struggles, of profit margins and compromises; it is a messy, twisted business that can drain the soul of a writer. It's just like *Speed the Plow*. Frank and I loved it. We found ourselves in this element and found that we were surprisingly good at manipulating it. Money was being thrown at us from a million different directions, and choices had to be made. Not that money was, at this point in our careers, much of an issue. We could have all lived comfortably, given our modest tastes (with the exception of Dirk) for years, just on the money we had made from the sales of our anthology. What we wanted was bigger than money. We wanted artistic control, which is worth far more than any bundle of cash.

Those first couple of weeks in L.A. were hairy. So many pretenders at every turn. Every night there was a different party that Marla told me was "absolutely critical" for me to attend. William went only to the first couple: a rather large affair hosted by the DreamWorks people and a wonderful day out at Coppola's ranch. Then William virtually disappeared, leaving Frank and I with the primary schmoozing duties. Dirk was, of course, attending parties of his own, hosted by celebrity members of the faithful: Tom Cruise, Simon LeBlanc, Tito Jackson, Clint Eastwood, people like that. But film was the furthest thing from their minds: they were hung up on theology.

I was worried about William, and I told Marla so. He had become mean and withdrawn. He abused waiters, waitresses, and stewardesses with a regularity that we had come to expect only from Dirk, who had become accustomed to being a living messiah with great expectations and a lot of "needs." I had not heard from William for nearly a week and a half when I had Marla track him down via his credit card receipts. They disturbed me. It looked as if he was having fun, but not the kind of fun you'd expect from William. To wit:

$2,250—Idle Wealth Speedway, San Luis Osbispo, CA
One-day rental of high performance automobile, track time.

$1,500—Swim With the Fishes Aquatic Adventures, Oakland, CA
Scuba diving with killer sharks in the shadow of the Golden Gate Bridge.

$2,000—Snowy Joe's Dry Cleaning, Compton, L.A., CA
Most likely a purchase of cocaine and/or crystal meth, or (highly improbable) stain removal from 142 dress shirts, as billed.

$1,555—Fly By Night Skydiving, Sonora, CA
Two midnight jumps (unassisted) from a turboprop at 3,500 feet.

$2,033—Trinity River Rafting
Three-day whitewater rafting expedition in Northern California. Solo.

$3,555—Stuntpower Institute
A weeklong course of stuntman study that included "Safely Falling From a Great Height," "Through Broken Glass Without Losing Your Ass," "Running Amid Explosions" and "The Doctor Is Out—Stitching Your Own Wounds."

I asked Marla to have the credit card company give me a call the next time anything popped up, and they did, and that is how I witnessed William's near-fatal, coma-inducing, bungie jumping accident in the Sierra Nevadas, at the Royal Gorge. It brings me pain even to think about it now.

I had supported the boys on their literary venture from day one, when they called me up in San Francisco one night when I had been fortunate enough to be having sex with an acquaintance whose name I can no longer recall. Certainly the whole business had seemed a trifle manic and disorganized, and I did have some very real apprehensions about being entangled in the affair, but on the whole it seemed to be a good thing. They were solid writers. I was proud of them for making good, and intended to help them as best I could.

It was at the opening of the film—its Hollywood premier—that I first began to notice that things were coming to a head, and, as a consequence, I was beginning to unravel. You see, I had never had occasion to meet Marla the publicist. And I had missed the wedding entirely. So when I entered the theater, attempting to feel as dignified as the tuxedo I wore, I saw for the first time Rettberg's wife.

And I felt a piece of myself crumble.

She and Rettberg were standing talking with Spielberg and hadn't noticed me yet, so I very coolly bought some popcorn and proceeded into the theater. At the very least, I intended to have myself an entertaining night at the movies. But, as it turned out, that is not what happened.

I must admit here that the film deal, despite being long-antic-ipated, had come as a surprise to me, but I took it in stride. I first found out about the Unknown film, in fact, the afternoon following the morning on which I had been interviewed by both *Poets and Writers* and *Wired* magazine. I had returned home from the two interviews, exhausted and overwhelmed by the adula-tion and the insincerity, and was seriously considering leaving the Unknown. It was then that I found the exuberant answering machine message from Rettberg, who had phoned from the new

Unknown offices in Chicago, where the three of them were well into their third bottle of champagne celebrating the signing of the film deal.

I had been involved early in the process of planning the film. At first, I had been quite earnest. You see, I had never had the opportunity to write a screenplay before, and was eager to try my hand at it. However, the process of developing the screenplay, during the time William was in the coma, seemed to primarily involve going to parties and meeting intoxicated celebrities, which I was admittedly not very good at. We drifted our separate ways. I was never sure whether I had given up on the process, or whether Rettberg and Stratton had given up on me. At the time, it seemed insignificant. I have never cared for Los Angeles, and things were going very well for me then at my position in San Francisco.

However, when I saw what had happened to what could have been a great film, I had a great many second thoughts.

I had, since my earliest boyhood, been an avid fan of the cinema. Upon reflection, I had never seen a film that I was not, to some degree, satisfied by. All of that was about to change.

Trying to force all thoughts of Rettberg's wife from my mind, I made my way into the theater and down the plush aisle toward the front row. The seats were full of people in tuxedos and evening gowns. They were chatting and laughing, and drinking Moet Chandon White Star champagne, which was being poured by impeccable wine stewards who moved up and down the aisles. There was the smell of swordfish being prepared for the appetizer. (There was to be a five-course gourmet meal served throughout the film.) I found myself a little put off by all this. I was, after all, a writer, and, as such, inhabited a different world than these people—the titans of Hollywood. I had always considered film as something secondary to literature—a tributary to the great river of literature, whose broad and powerful currents had flowed for hundreds of years. Film, I had always thought, existed to make literature richer. The thought that things were the other way around left rather a bad taste in my mouth.

I found myself alone in the first row. I suspected that I was the only one here to see the film, and that everyone else was here to be seen seeing the film by such-and-such famous director or other. Again, I tried to force these cynical thoughts from my mind, and tried to enjoy the popcorn. I found, though, that it had been flavored with some kind of garlic butter with capers, and, I suspected, tri-color pepper. It had a hint of anchovy. I briefly considered returning to the concessions stand and demanding normal popcorn, but quickly subdued my irritation. I was here to see a movie, I reminded myself, nothing more.

At last the film began.

The opening scene was set in a bookstore. The camera panned slowly over an anthology shelf. A quick scrutiny of the titles revealed to me that they were not real books—they were spines designed by studio professionals to resemble real books—and there was not a single anthology I recognized, nor did I see anything published by Norton or Sun and Moon Press. I found this bothered me for reasons I could not put a finger on. Finally the camera rose upward and, in a shot facing downward, panned over the tops of the shelves. The effect was admittedly stunning—that of floating across the ceiling of a bookstore looking down; as I had imagined the ghost of Kerouac had so often done.

The camera now descended to take in a man in a trenchcoat standing in an aisle reading. Because the man wore sunglasses and his face was concealed behind a screen of smoke from the cigarette he inhaled from obsessively (in a bookstore?), it took me a moment to recognize Willem DaFoe. The camera abruptly shifted focus as, behind DaFoe, the doors of the store opened and four figures strode in wearing sunglasses. The man in the trenchcoat slowly put the book away and turned to face the newcomers.

The man in the trenchcoat said, "Bill."

A tight close-up of the mouth of one of the people entering the store revealed a sinister frown, and the man spit the words "Don't call me that, Vollman." The camera zoomed out to reveal that the actor who spoke was none other than Tom Cruise. The camera then panned over the faces of the other men: James Spader (as Rettberg?), Sean Connery (Dirk??), Tom Cruise (with platform shoes) (William???), and Dustin Hoffman (me!?).

My heart sank.

There then ensued a fistfight between Tom Cruise as William and Willem DaFoe as, I reasoned, William Vollman. This fight was very brutal and not at all literary. The sight of Cruise repeatedly punching DaFoe's face as blood splattered across some set designer's idea of an anthology section, each punch sounding like a sledgehammer on gravel, a rock song I recognized as by the Tragically Hip rising to deafening volume on the theater's 32-speaker Dolby surround sound, all filled me with a peculiar realization: that literature was indeed dead, supplanted by commercial sensationalism. And that I, and every other writer who took themselves seriously, was doomed to wander America as a sort of ghost.

After the two and a half hours of automatic weapons, high-speed car chases, incessant rock and roll, biceps, bikinis, cigarettes, and hard liquor, I was wild with exasperation. As the credits rolled and the crowd applauded and whistled and cheered, I stormed out into the lobby, determined to have words with Rettberg.

I moved through the crowd but could find neither him nor the other Unknown writers. Pushing my way into the men's room, I was greeted by the sight of men in tuxedos passing mirrors. Fighting the urge to knock their blasted cocaine to the floor, I shouted, "Rettberg! Rettberg!"

The next thing I knew I was being roughly escorted to the street by two muscular bouncers. They threw me out onto the Sunset Strip and the theater doors fell closed and locked.

As I stood up and brushed myself off, inside the lobby, I caught sight of Marla. She was kissing Dustin Hoffman on both cheeks and everybody was laughing.

At that moment, I understood that I was to live out the rest of my empty years as a broken man.

I remember this night. It was the crescendo of our spiral of self-destructive behavior. I don't remember anything for weeks before, and the period afterward is a confused blur.

Dirk had taken too much acid in too short a time, and required almost half a sheet to get off. A reader had traded (for copies of the anthology) a lot of mescaline in microdot form. We were being swept toward the falls by a vicious undertow, we could all feel it, and so we swam with the current. Dirk spilled the vial and tiny blue red and green dots rolled all over the glass coffee table. Frank, William, and I scrambled to collect the tiny pellets before they were lost to the carpet in confusion. We each ate a great many without consideration. As the three of us scraped the table with our hands, practically licking it, collecting in our cupped palms microdots, ashes, cocaine and beer residue, shake, roaches, lint, eating all of it, Dirk, realizing what happened, screamed and drove his leg down through the glass face of the coffee table in a spray of microdots and broken glass.

We rolled away from the table and Dirk stood there stunned, his pant leg torn.

There was already blood.

We could feel the madness surge through the tiny room like we were immersed in a rapid flood of adrenaline.

Dirk began to crawl around looking for microdots in a shag carpet littered with glass shards, pills, and cigarette butts.

This was a near-impossible task for a man in his condition, and, as he grunted, we watched, nervous.

Frank stood up and sat on the bed and picked up the remote and turned on CNN.

There was a story about air strikes in Kosovo.

William stood up next, and walked unsteadily to the tiny refrigerator, whose supply of tiny bottles of whiskey and liqueur we had almost erased.

He pulled out a tiny bottle of Dewars, unscrewed and drained it, tossed it aside.

He pulled out a tiny bottle of Johnny Walker Red Label, unscrewed and drained it, tossed it aside.

He pulled out a tiny bottle of Oban, unscrewed and drained it, tossed it aside.

I lit a cigarette without taking my eyes off Dirk.

He had the fever. I could see it.

He might, at any moment, break furniture, cry, or recite *To The Lighthouse*, which he had an uncanny ability to do when intoxicated beyond any peninsula of reason in the deep and deadly tides of sensation.

William opened a can of Tucher Hefe-Weizen.

He was trying to remember where we had put the marijuana. Good. We needed something to mellow the vibe.

Fast.

Then I heard a toilet flush and a shriek from the bathroom.

William, still looking around for the marijuana, went to the bathroom, and tried the door.

It was locked.

Frank screamed again.

"What is it?" William yelled, pounding on the door.

NATO troops were bombing former Yugoslavia.

Frank's voice was shrill: "Deconstructionism!" He screamed again.

William began to kick the door.

Dirk looked upset.

I felt that it was time for my next fix and I wished Frank would leave the bathroom.

It was unknown how many casualties there had been so far.

William kicked the door down and ran into the bathroom where Frank was crying loudly.

Dirk stood up.

"Let's have some marijuana, how about? It'll mellow us out," I offered, shaking.

Dirk sat on the bed.

"Where's the boo, Dirk?"

"DERRIDA! DERRRRRRRRIDAAAAAAAAAAAAAAA!!"

"It's cool, Frank, it's cool. Derrida isn't here, man, there's no theory here, man."

President Clinton said something about Democracy.

Dirk opened his suitcase, took out a revolver, and shot the television.

The first bullet missed. Plaster fell from the wall.

The second bullet made the screen go black.

Clinton explained how Serbia had destabilized the region.

The third bullet silenced him.

The fourth bullet basically tore the set apart.

There were, I reasoned, two bullets left. There was some anxiety.

Dirk looked troubled. He was pointing the revolver at the scorched wall where the TV had been.

Frank was throwing up blood.

William, oblivious, covered with Frank's vomit, stumbled back to the refrigerator, walking through Dirk's line of fire.

He opened a can of Fosters.

"Dirk," I suggested, "let's call room service for a pizza."

What Frank Said:

—We should be subservient to the needs of the state. The state's bigger, means more. I'm a believer in nationalism. But one worldwide nationalism, not individual ones. The state is the earth, the galaxy. Its populations are like its internal organs, and they need to function together, like a huge ecosystem. We're too many people. We can break, we can be reborn. It's not a problem to give birth to a million babies, it happens all the time. Not one person, but a lot of people, a lot of pregnant women. Straight lines, right angles, everything white, and top-down command structures. You know what I'm saying. This is bullshit, so what, I'm fucked up. Fuck you, you want to fight me on this one? You want to get your ass kicked?

Frank's eyes rolled up into his head, disappearing for nine minutes. When they fell back down, they were beet-red and manic. Frank began rubbing them. Then he leaned back and was snoring.

There was only one thing we agreed on: we were rabid socialists to a man. Red lions, given to rallying and stein-clashing. We lived by slogans. We would baffle Republicans with our ironfisted proclamations that the United States of America was a socialist state to the core, and always had been. Question was: at whose expense? Free land to white men, immigrant labor. But if someone triggered Dirk's sentiments over Southern Comfort, he might rail from a barstool, waving a copy of *Herland*. Public transportation, national parks and libraries. We knew that experimental literature owed a lot to public funding: public universities and their presses, the NEA, the IAC, and, and we cannot stress this enough, public libraries. State-funded repositories of state-funded lit. Curt White had a job and could afford to write, and we couldn't be happier. A few authors manage to stay out of academe: DeLillo, Auster, Gaddis, McCarthy, but they are increasingly the exception. Not that being deep-fried in theory has a positive effect on everyone's writing. When we founded the Unknown, Rettberg was working for Amoco, and I had been proofreading speeches of football coaches (an impossible job, given that even the name of the publishing company I worked for had a typo in it, and no proofreader who wants to keep working would dare point out a fact like that [Coaches Choice—no apostrophe]). We were raving, man. Our project depended on the state and that was as it should be. We were fucking writing the literature to usher America into the Second Millennium. America had a hypertext that was being browsed worldwide. There were rumors that Scholes had a paper in the works about us. Because we were the shit. We were good old Yankee know-how applied to the electronic medium of the next thousand years. We were American, we were making the most of it, because America was the wealthiest, mightiest, and most wretched and disliked and humiliated and self-loathing nation on earth.

Scott had that special way about him. Dirk was different, Dirk wrote poetry. Scott and William were both in awe and intensely suspicious of Dirk's ability to do that.

"It's about death," Dirk would say, "and language. And most of all, it's about itself, because poetry is about itself."

William would look at Scott and Scott would look at William and then both would look at Dirk to see whether he was joking. Dirk was never joking and so William and Scott tried not to look like they thought he might be joking.

Then the subject might turn to Scott's fiction—"it's a voice that I heard in my head"—or William's—"I tried to use every verb tense once per paragraph. It seems like it's stream-of-consciousness but it really isn't." Some people thought the Unknown wasn't really about the writing so much. And some followers—the sort who might read about their exploits in the *New York Observer*—even developed theories. "It was Rettberg's outspokenness that eventually won the public over." Or "A lot has been made about the Unknown's relationship with drugs, but Dirk was really the only one who was a compulsive user."

But Scott had that special way about him. "Make it bigger, goddamn it, that's just a poem," he might say, "and to hell with the typos. The kids of today love reading our typos."

At the end of the Far North American wing of the tour, in Anchorage, we had been driving for so long that we no longer looked, smelled, nor acted human. There was nothing to read but Louis L'Amour at the Vancouver Hilton. The tape deck, somewhere outside of Vancouver, jammed so that it could no longer eject the tape, which was *Are You Experienced?* backed with *Purple Rain*.

We gave a great show in Anchorage. I remember that I humped a shelf of kids' books, moaning obscenely, while Scott read the "Meddlesome Passenger," while simultaneously playing an electric guitar solo, or maybe I imagined the electric guitar solo. Dirk read part of the *New Modern Library Edition Gertrude Stein Reader*, and then he set it on fire and knelt down before the burning trade paperback, gesticulating erotically, as the crowd looked on baffled.

We spent a little jail time in Anchorage.

By this point, I had begun pontificating at such a volume, flailing my arms about, that the other patrons of the Cyber A Cafe had begun to regard me with visible discomfort.

"Dirk," I proclaimed, "if there is anything I detest so much as Southern California—its choking traffic, luxury-encrusted boutique and condominium-denigrated coastline, its vacuous glassy-eyed and repellent denizens and the neurotic hypocrisy of their restrained suburban violence—it is computers. Computers, Dirk, are the most outrageous travesty of the twentieth century. Nothing has more thoroughly sucked the humanity from the human world than computers. Computers have substituted for human interaction, intelligent conversation, and the free play of body and intellect an abhorrent pixilated grid. Thanks to computers, Dirk, thinkers, poets, and composers have been supplanted by a despicable digerati of sexually malnourished, emotionally stunted, video blinded, keyboard numbed petit bourgeoisie."

Dirk opened his mouth to pose an interjection, but, although my tirade was rapidly becoming intolerable even to myself, I relentlessly continued with my philosophizing disquisition. "The person who invented the blog, Dirk, is guilty of the most egregious crime against language one could possibly commit, the most heinous, unforgivable, malevolent, stupid, noxious, unremittingly vicious, sociopathic, brutal, insipid, flagrant, odious, astringent, barbaric, puerile, inhumane, chauvinistic, Medieval, unsympathetic, tortuous, torturous, alienating, spiritually carcinogenic..."

At this point I lost consciousness.

The mountains themselves objects of fascination. The mountains too part of the unknown. The sense of perspective becomes outrageous. The air which is thinner but more clean. Actual snowcaps. Scott and William come from Illinois. Geography there purely a matter of slight rolls in the flatness. Most hills there formed by bulldozers. The mountains describe a feeling. There, nature makes its presence known. Away from the ski resorts and the trinket parlors of the nouveau riche, birds of prey and pine trees and rare fungi reach up to a place where there is tundra, and there are no voices. Here in the mountains, all is not known. But serene, serene. All parts under trailing stars, everything breathing.

Mike was eager to be our chauffeur through Colorado. He had written some of my lines, I had rewritten some of his sentences, and he was a great researcher and avid reader of the news. Which is not even to mention a swell guy, a pal's pal. One of the kindest party-throwing militant communists in Urbana (who had hosted the fabulous outdoor barbecue at which we had first met Barbara Trent, who, much later, after Dirk's assassination and the whole Y2K upheaval, would do the documentary film: *The Unknown: Exposed*), Mike was a skilled offroader and drove a '93 Isuzu Rodeo with the 31.5 inch big tire package, locking differential, and the five-speed manual, 4.31 final drive gear ratio.

We knew that we liked Mike's model narrow-gauge railroad. What we didn't know was that he drove like a nuclear missile up the asshole of hell. Like fire on fire, or a swarm of hornets, like Chuck Yeager, upside down, across vistas that would make your stomach turn if you were from the flatlands, which we were and which it did. One slip of the tire would have meant any of our deaths, but, as he drove, he managed to keep our beers full from the keg of Heineken bolted in between the seats. That was what scared us the most actually: the idea that that badly shaken keg might explode. But Mike had a special knack for handling good beer at high altitudes. He hardly lost a shred of foam. And he was an exceptional host, considering that we were in a truck.

There's usually trouble with lighting dope at that altitude. Mike had a torch and knew the path and drove like a studied maniac. He knew the path and it scared us, but he always bucked those cliffs and got the wheels back on the road through determined gravity. He blasted Bob Marley.

Dirk got sick first.

Frank was there. He told me that it would be okay. We'd reach the border and we'd be back on the book tour as usual. This was worse than a bad review, all this hanging on the edges of cliffs on two wheels, one wheel, as Mike tore through some sense-mutilating curves along precipices that made everyone, to a man, almost pee his pants. But what a driver!

And what a terrain. Those red gorges, rocky jagged upheavals, horrible crags, and the old narrow-gauge line where the strike was, where those workers were gunned down and their blood ran red like the rocks and dust and flag. We were almost choked with our love for America, the land trod by those weird people who loved our writing, those Americans so desperate for literature that they missed Bukowski and avoided the newspaper. Choked by patriotism as we burned rubber between the rocks of the land those pale immigrants stole from the indigenous peoples by inventing land ownership, a psychotic concept they enforced with violence. All four of the Unknown in the backseats were choked by fear as the Isuzu bounded like a gazelle from rock to rock. A 3400-pound ballerina, camo-green, snarling and swigging gasoline like a revolutionary poet.

Scott got sick third.

Frank was there to comfort me during my sickness. We're gonna die, Frank, man, he's a good driver, but he's in trouble tonight I know it. No way, Frank said. Just think about Dickens. Think about Stein. *Tender Buttons*, William, think about that. Think about Marx. After all, it's just an internal combustion engine. Think about Camus. Wait, don't think about Camus, Camus died in a car crash, think about Woolf, think about Howling Wolf.

And then the storm began. We had just reached the shelf road below the final tangent up to Cinnamon Pass. It's a narrow trail, clinging to a mass of earth and rockslide constantly shifting downhill. Occasionally, a US Forest Service road grader would struggle over, attempting to level the ever-shifting road. You had to actually look at the road before you started across it. If you encountered anyone coming down the trail, you did have the right of way; uphill traffic always did. But did you really want to watch someone back off the trail to their certain deaths? But we were in a hurry.

Just then hailstones began to pelt down from the threatening, swirling clouds. Lightning struck all around us and then began to hit below us! Mike simply stopped in the middle of the trail. "I can't see where we're going! We'll have to risk that no one is stupid enough to try going downhill in this storm," he shouted, as the beating of hailstones on the roof of the truck drowned out everything except the Blue Öyster Cult's "Secret Treaties." We sat there for a few minutes and passed the bowl, loaded with hashish and opium. The smoke filled the truck, relieving our anxiety. Soon, we could make out a winter-like scene, with the terrain, fantastic already, now covered in a white blanket a few inches thick. You would have to ski in or rent a helicopter to drop you off to get here in the winter and still you would risk setting off an avalanche to see such a vista. Mike simply engaged second gear, low range, and continued up the hill, past the snowbank that delineated the top of the pass.

"Glaciers," Mike said, "glaciers."

What, I thought, did he mean by "Glaciers?"

Then I thought about the malleable nature of perception, and I thought about the Jesus Paper in Dirk's shaving kit. But I couldn't think about that. The thought that Mike was negotiating this hazardous topography under the influence of hallucinogens made me uncomfortable. Seeing glaciers. We ripped over the foothills of Cinnamon Mountain and the descending sun burned orange in a narrow aperture of cloud. "Glaciers," Mike said, "the next Ice Age, fellas, hope I can outrun it."

Mike began then, in desperation, to assemble his portable blender, which plugged into the Isuzu's dashboard cigarette lighter, and handed it to Dave, in the passenger's seat. Mike steered with his teeth as he opened a can of coconut milk and then a can of pineapple juice, handing each to Dave to pour into the blender. Lastly, ice, from the glove-compartment refrigerator, and a lime deftly chopped into quarters on the dashboard by Mike, with one hand on the wheel and the other wielding his nine-inch dark-bladed survival knife. It seemed to absorb the lightning it was so black. It was freaky. There was that knife and the intermittent hum of the blender.

Things had begun, for me, to dissolve into a blur of undifferentiated sensation. The opium and hashish had begun to soften me. My tongue was like good leather and cloves. I was above myself, peaceful, mellow, enjoying the distant reggae, a flow of oil lubricating dry and corroded arteries. Endorphins waltzing with adrenaline, the truck a grand dance-hall, with frescoed ceiling and chandelier. Warm jets of pleasure gushed from my joints. Rain beat on the windshield, dissolving the fragment of red sunset. Lightning described a complicated figure.

A jolt. Mike braked and slid to a stop, tires carving a quartet of deep streaks in the wet gravel. Before us, revealed in the lightning's sinister flash, a ghost town. The buildings seemed empty, but foreboding.

Presence hinted otherwise. Mike switched off the engine and there was the roar of the storm. And the ticking of the cooling engine. And the drum of raindrops. Then he shut down the headlights and there was only the burning orange comma of the hooter, connecting our clauses and slowly scrawling a constellation of the six men in the truck's interior.

The building was dark and shadows moved therein. We saw the weak glow of mining helmet lanterns. We saw figures. And then in a flash they went down in the street their torsos blooming red in the splash of bullets. And men in suits with false badges lowered their rifles. Thunder.

And then the rain and the dark and none of us breathing not a one—

"What the hell was that," asked Frank, "what was that, did you see that?"

"Ghosts," said Mike, "ghosts of the miners, the striking miners, gunned down by company goons. 1915. I saw it."

And another flash revealing nothing. And then the radio coming on, even though Mike hadn't touched the dashboard, even though we were out of range of any station, playing Phil Ochs playing "Joe Hill."

Something strange had just happened.

As if thousands of struggling workers and artists had cried out in pain and were suddenly silenced.

The next day we planted lots of grass in the Colorado mountains and felt better.

We thought that the next Unknown anthology could be a little red songbook.

Scott Rettberg's Testimony, U.S. vs. Barnes & Noble

Prosecutor: Your Honor, I'd like to call to the stand on behalf of my clients, Mr. Scott Rettberg, webmaster of the Mining Company Guide to Authors, and part-time hypertext novelist.

Judge Ris: Proceed.

Rettberg: Your Honor, I won't dick you around—

Defense: Objection!

Judge Ris: Overruled.

Rettberg: Look, your Honor, I smoke and drink and lie, I won't make excuses. But I work hard, your Honor, and I live in this country so I can pursue my dream. My dream has always been the same, my dream is the most important thing to me, my dream is simple: I want to get published.

[Cheering from the gallery. Judge reestablishes order.]

Rettberg: I just want a shot at being like those guys who made this country what it is by giving it a literature, your Honor. Those guys who sat down in the middle of this big land of opportunity, right when everybody else was grabbing land and panning gold and getting great buffalo-skin rugs, who wrote books and drank and starved and went insane and shot themselves, when everybody else was out shooting other people.

Guys like: Emily Dickenson, Sylvia Plath, Audrey Lorde, Adrienne Rich, Carolyn Forché, bell hooks, June Jordan, May Swenson, and Eve Merriam, guys with guts and something to say and good grammar.

Take a look at the way things were in this country before Herman Melville: we had slavery, women weren't allowed to vote, and there were no cars or electricity. And then came Melville.

And today we have electricity.

Did these guys think about becoming rich off of oil or steel or agriculture or copper or software? Did these guys think about getting rich off of publishing?

[Commotion in the courtroom.]

Of course they did, your Honor, they thought about a lot of things. But instead of doing them, they wrote books.

And now, Barnes & Noble, your Honor, has bought up Ingram like so many overstock copies of *A Frolic of His Own.*

[Marquardt whooping from the courtroom floor. Judge reestablishes order.]

One company wants to single-handedly rule the bookselling and distribution and eventually the publishing industries. In this "land of opportunity."

One company, your Honor, a single corporate interest, wants to be the sole mediator between writer and reader.

One set of stockholders will now make decisions that will affect all of American literature, scholarship, and journalism for years to come.

One corporation will rule every piece of writing in this country, I reckon, except hypertext novels.

Now is Uncle Sam going to stop this, so guys like me and my buddies in the Unknown can live our simple dream, a fair dream, and say what we want to say, and see who's listening?

Is Uncle Sam going to help us get our writing onto paper so people can read it on the train going to work at Citibank or Jean's Place?

Or is Uncle Sam going to take advantage of the situation? And take those writers like me and William, who use our First Amendment rights for their sole intended purpose, and fuck us like roasted pigs on a sharp wooden stick on the Fourth of July?

[Silence on the floor.]

(Pardon me, your Honor.)

Thank you, your Honor, ladies and gentlemen of the courtroom and jury, Frank.

[The crowd goes wild.]

When we were in D.C., we got an interesting offer from CIA director George Tenet. He had heard us reading from *The Unknown* on Ollie North's radio show, and had decided to hire us. He spoke to us over the phone and said that it was an insecure line so he couldn't go into any detail.

He had us meet our handler, who went by the name of "Cormac McCarthy," at the Borders. In the Political Science section, we were approached by an overweight man in an impeccable suit and mirrored Ray Bans. "I like Stephen King," he offered. Dirk said: "William here likes language poetry, but Scott here likes metafiction." This was the proper response. The man laughed and shook our hands vigorously. "My name is Cormac. Our friend in San Francisco says you boys write good." This was obviously a veiled reference to Frank. This stunned us. Was Frank a spook? We didn't know he had ties.

Over croissants at the Borders Café, Cormac spoke openly to us about his plan. The CIA was to finance a special cut-out, code-named the Unknown. We would be foreign operatives. Our purpose would be to infiltrate Eastern European literary circles in order to get close to burgeoning Eastern European politicians.

We listened to his plan with interest....

We were taken in a van with tinted windows and government insignia to a small airfield.

I expressed to Cormac my concern that he was flying us out of the country before we'd been able to meet the Clintons, who were all big fans of *The Unknown*, even Chelsea, even Roger, who reportedly howled with laughter at our comical fictional drug-fueled book tour during his stay at the Betty Ford Clinic. Cormac winked. "The Clintons are going to be more happy to see you now than ever, now that they know you're going to help us out on our little project overseas." Did this mean that we were involved in a covert operation that not only the President, but the First Lady, were aware of? We didn't realize that we were going to be reporting so high up. Maybe we were bypassing the CIA altogether.

Cormac escorted us to a C-123. We climbed inside and tried to make ourselves comfortable. Outside on the runway, soldiers were loading gigantic crates onto our plane. It occurred to me to be apprehensive. Dirk was reading John Ashbery and was withdrawn. Scott was smoking and fixing martinis. He saw me looking and smiled and said, "It's on Uncle Sam." Just then, a man I assumed was the pilot came back to where we were sitting. He had a white helmet and jumpsuit—no military markings— and orange goggles. He looked stern and Scott was about to ask if it was okay to smoke inside the plane when the stubble on the man's cleft chin wiggled into a smile and he lifted his goggles and it was Frank.

We were surprised as hell and all smiles and backslapping but what the fuck? Frank could pilot a C-123? He sure didn't pick up that knowledge when we were working on our master's degrees back in Normal. It was a liberal arts program, we didn't learn any applicable skills. And he couldn't have joined the armed forces in 1997 and be working for intelligence, very high-level, in 1999. So he must have been working for the CIA or the NSC or (I shuddered) the DEA the whole time when we were in grad school together. Even when I snuck that hit of marijuana when I was studying Kristeva in his kitchen and he smelled it. Frank the Spook. Marine Lieutenant Colonel Marquardt. Which was undoubtedly only one of many aliases.

But why would an intelligence operative get a creative writing degree? To spy on someone. And that someone could be only one person.

Krass-Mueller.

We were in Serbia's restless Kosovo province staring at the floor of a hangar housing a factory that manufactured untraceable parts for automatic weapons. There were machines and workers. When we asked who the weapons were for, "Cormac" told us, "You guys don't have a need to know." Then William asked what he was there to do. "I'm used to fiction workshops, so tell me how many pages, how many copies, and give me a deadline," he said, and this was a joke, but "Cormac" didn't get it.

Across the hangar, the C-123 was being unloaded. From out of the strange crates came stacks of money and bags of an unidentified white substance.

"Cormac" said, "The Agency recruited you because of your manufacturing expertise. Our men in the field have been having trouble with weapons jamming when they get hot after being on automatic for awhile."

We looked at each other. "But we're writers," we said, "we don't know anything about manufacturing."

"Cormac" suddenly went pale and nervous. "You're what?" he stammered.

The project was aborted and we were back in D.C. in time for dinner with the Clintons that evening. Chelsea had flown in from Stanford just to meet us.

Turns out that "Cormac" had confused Operation Bookworm with Operation Metal Octopus, and we had been flown to Serbia instead of Prague. He said it would take a couple of days to straighten everything out, and gave us an envelope containing one hundred hundred-dollar bills to kill time in D.C. He winked: "We'll contact you again in a few days. Until then, have a good time on Uncle. Think of it as an NEA grant." He said that our new contact went by the name of "Mark Twain." Twain, he said, would be in touch soon enough. He reminded us not to write about what we had seen in Serbia. "Of course not," William lied, "we write straight fiction."

A year later, looking back on this, I began to wonder whether William's bungie-jumping accident had, in fact, been an accident. And Dirk's assassination?

We weren't sure where to have fun in D.C. We tried to look up Marion Barry, but he was unlisted.

Newt Gingrich had also heard us on Ollie North's radio show and called the hotel (how had he known which hotel? I guess the Speaker of the House probably has ways of knowing) to invite us out for Long Island Iced Tea and shrimp scampi. He knew a very "exclusive" (what did this mean? No Blacks? No Jews? No Democrats?) seafood place.

All our preconceptions were wrong, friends, because the Right it is a-changin'. We had expected to meet any of several small, slender, often brightly-colored salamanders of the genus *Triturus* and related genera, living chiefly on land but becoming aquatic during the breeding season, whose "Contract for America" had seemed like a war on America's poor (the 90 percent of the population who owned 10 percent of the wealth loved our anthology, while the richest 10 percent loved our hypertext). Instead we arrived at a Cajun club with very loud jazz and a mostly African-American clientele. Newt's congressional limo had been very conspicuous parked outside on a street of abandoned warehouses and broken glass. We found him dancing right below the stage. He was wearing a lei, loud Bermuda shorts, and heart-shaped rose-colored sunglasses.

We got about fifty shrimp dipped in coconut batter and served with a Thai peanut sauce. Newt wouldn't let us eat anything else, it was out of the question, this was his favorite dish. And we were going to drink pitchers of strawberry margaritas, made with fresh strawberries, Cuervo Gold, and Grand Marnier. With extra lime. A drink he was nuts about. And he couldn't stop talking about the hypertext.

We were ribbing him about Clinton and the whole health care thing, and El Shifa, the Sudanese pharmaceutical factory Clinton had bombed, and the Lewinski thing (which, even a year later, you couldn't stop hearing about, as if the whole thing were just an elaborate plot—a staged scandal—wrought by covert black operatives to get all the people of America to get fed up and stop reading or watching or listening to the news altogether, so a secret government could subvert the Y2K election and plant an operative in power [which theory, Newt, basically, admitted was true]). We made him laugh so hard that margarita came out his nose.

Even though the restaurant didn't seem like his kind of place, it was obvious he was appreciated there. He tipped big. He seemed to have lots of African-American friends. He was getting paid top dollar as a lobbyist and he was happy in his retirement.

We had been so wrong about him.

Sure his "Contract for America" was a war on the poor, but he was a lot more charismatic than we had expected. Plus, he picked up the tab. "On Uncle," he said.

We were nervous about meeting Ollie North, but there was no reason to be. He hosted a successful D.C. radio show, and his days as an architect of secret government were clearly over. He had been on TV, he was exposed, he took a fall, he resigned, and he didn't go to jail for even a day. Now he chatted it up with guests, read ad copy, gave harmless editorials, and talked about his favorite restaurants. He interviewed us about our book, and said it made him proud to be an American.

We wondered what he meant.

"Frank, have another Corona, and tell me: what were you doing in Normal. You were working for Uncle Sam then, right?"

"Oh, I can't really discuss that."

"Come on, man, we let you into the Unknown. Fill us in on what you know."

"Well, let's say I was in training for Operation Bookworm. The CIA was paying my expenses there so I could learn to write cutting-edge fiction and become famous in Eastern Europe. Then I would infiltrate literary circles so that the CIA could manipulate popular opinion and plant some of our boys both in office and in the publishing houses. We're going to start a fully-legitimate publishing house as a cover, and we need skilled editors such as yourselves to run the show down there.

"Once the house is successful and prosperous, we're going to use it to launder money from our other operations. Think of it: if the Unknown suddenly has a couple extra million dollars in their account, none of the bankers will bat an eye because you boys are so darn successful. To them it'll just look like you gave a reading and got paid in cash. And you will have access to lots of funds with which you can publish many Unknown anthologies, without worrying about losing money on the venture. This will give the whole black operation an air of legitimacy. And you will send many many boxes of the Unknown anthologies back to the U.S. via Southern Air Transport and Air America, two of our airlines. This to ensure no problems in customs. Shall I just say that we may be transporting some extracts from Asian flowers along with the anthologies, through our proprietary supplier in Russia."

"Is the KGB in on this?"

"You don't have a need to know."

"What were you doing in Normal, Frank, for real? Were you spying on Krass-Mueller?"

"Let's just say that he had some very important connections in the literary community."

While we were in D.C., we decided to fly Adam in and have him take some promotional photos for future hypertext novels and book jackets. He suggested we take some shots in front of DEA Headquarters. We thought that was a fine idea. We did not, at the time, consider ourselves recreational users. We were professionals. And this fact, thanks to the war on drugs, made us martyrs of a sort. So we felt we owed the DEA for being narcs, busting users, locking up artists, and, in general, making us into heroes and rebels.

We were in the park across the street trying to line up a shot that included the face of the DEA Headquarters along with the flags when a few suits came out and started to approach us. It was at this point that I realized that I was holding. It just hadn't occurred to me to leave the marijuana in the car for the DEA shoot. I started sweating. The suits walked up, wingtips impeccable. They had mirrored shades. Looked like one of them was packing a .33 in an ankle holster. The other one looked mean and he was reaching inside his jacket, his hand moving toward his shoulder. My knees turned to theory. I wanted to run. He pulled his hand out of his jacket wielding a copy of *The Unknown: An Anthology*.

Autographs. They wanted autographs.

They turned out to be great guys and they took us out drinking. They were pros, too, it turned out. Rourke had been working twelfth floor under the marijuana desk for about three years. South was about to go undercover in Illinois, and this day had been the last day he would spend behind a desk for many weeks. We tried to get him to talk about his project, and we eventually, many rounds later, did get him to talk. We're fiction writers, we said, except Dirk, we're expert liars. Even if we tried to expose your mission, it would just be literature, it wouldn't be a threat to you.

Turns out that there was a certain celebrated metafictionist in Illinois whom the DEA knew had previous ties to some big dealers in the Boston area. South had enrolled in a master's program to try to get close to him. To pull off the cover, he had had to read a lot of John Barth in a short time, in order to be a convincing graduate student.

This was too much. I pulled Scott aside and we played pinball. I expressed my concern:

"South is about to embark on a mission that has already failed. Not only is he going to get an advanced degree in English Studies, he's going after a man who's cleaned up his life and lost his connections. A professor. He's going to Normal, Illinois. We should tell him to call it off."

Scott skewered me with a skeptical glance. "South is a great guy, but he's a narc. Narcs suck. Let him bang his head against a wall. Maybe he'll end up reading Thomas Pynchon and learn a little about life."

I saw his point. So we let the narc have it. Then we went to dinner.

Dinner with the Clintons was a lot of fun. Swordfish steaks with herb butter and capers. Moet Chandon White Star champagne. Potatoes au gratin.

Though there was a certain tension. Despite her charisma, we got the feeling that Hillary was mad at Bill about something. Chelsea had to act as a go-between.

After mousse and espresso with Bailey's Irish Cream, President Clinton started to open up to us, and tell us about his favorite authors. Chelsea looked uncomfortable and tried to change the subject but without success. Turns out that Clinton was big into Updike. I couldn't think of anything to say, since I hate Updike. Clinton had read almost every John Irving book. And he considered Raymond Carver a genius. Scott tried to steer him onto the topic of DeLillo. Clinton had read *Iron John* and it clearly was an important text for him. Hillary excused herself. Frank's eyes were glazing over. Clinton was a big fan of thrillers as well, he explained, citing Crichton, Clancy, Grisham, Koontz. Dirk looked at his watch. Chelsea finished the Bailey's, hiccuped, and made a crack about a book called *Chicken Soup for the Chief Executive's Soul*. Bill looked hurt but defiant. For a second I thought he was going to go get his *Bible*.

But Frank pulled out a copy of *The Unknown: An Anthology* and saved the evening with a dynamic reading of the D.C. sequence. Hillary came back and we ended up having a great time, downing a full seven bottles of champagne. On Uncle.

Bing bang boom baby and smokestacks yeah as we drive down the wide street this cat is blowing this sax there and the music is like zen steeped in boiling fog and me and Scott and Dirk are three dilated eyeballs soaking in the benzedrine gin floating in glasses like orange shapes the cigarette sketches out the details of against the night. Scott needs a drink and I feel a poem coming on and a slow train is like the clicking of a piano and in this jazz lounge we run into Frank by accident. This cosmic coincidence has completed the trilogy of reason and hare rama hare hare wow zippety do dah day. Then Frank runs out on the street like Groucho Marx smoking a hooter and batting his eyelashes crazily at passersby of the night. There is a star in the sky that has burned through eternity and a wave of delirium tremens flows over me like a wave of colonial invaders over a peaceful continent Christianizing my cells and taxing them we go puddling through mountain driving baby see city lights yeah see gargantuan airports no oh frontierymeweewee pudda ludda bodda buddha bing bang boom.

J.D. Salinger, apparently, was always late for these things. But Alice B. Toklas was an exceptional surprise. Ms. Toklas is quite old, but her hashish brownies are still the best anywhere.

I was playing shuffleboard with Paul Auster, who was quite vicious. He cheated, and when I accused him of cheating, he got very red.

Much later he would seek revenge.

But everything turned out all right.

Krass-Mueller finally read the hypertext. Although the acutely self-conscious literary figure and internet-phobe's first response was to kick a hole through the wall, yell, and throw a copy of *Blood Meridian* at his dog, a couple of weeks later he admitted that it was pretty funny, and said that he was reconsidering his initial threat to sue us.

Dirk and Scott, surprisingly, put their doctoral degrees (ABD's actually) and their vast knowledge of critical theory to work to end the war in Kosovo, calling for an end to "identity politics bullshit." Now, schoolchildren in Kosovo, regardless of their ethnicity, take mandatory Albanian and Serbian history and language classes, and ethnic strife is already far less severe in Yugoslavia than in Chicago.

And Paul Auster called me up to apologize for cheating at shuffleboard. To make it up to me, he invited me to New York for a game of Trivial Pursuit and a little "friendly wagering." I am pretty sure that the deck of Trivial Pursuit cards was rigged, though. I discovered this when Auster landed on Art & Literature, I drew a card, and asked him "What characteristic of Juliet did Romeo believe might 'kill the envious moon'?" Auster answered "thermonuclear fusion," which was in fact the answer printed on the card, but a quick glance at the Riverside Shakespeare (and at first Auster tried to deny owning any Shakespeare) proved that this answer was not correct. Finally, I looked through the cards and found a number of suspiciously difficult questions:

Q: Who was the first nonmilitary Swede to receive the honor of Knight of the First Order of the Polar Star?

A: Carl Linnaeus

Q: Which pharmaceutical and timber company stockholder launched the first anti-hemp campaign?

A: William Randolph Hearst

Q: Who coined the phrase, "All you arts screw to the highest?"

A: Kenneth Gaburo

And the devastatingly hard:

Q: Wer wurde am drei Dezember achtzehn hundert drei und achtzig in Wien geboren?

A: Anton Webern

After I forced him to confess, Auster again apologized for cheating.

But his tone of voice sounded like he was swearing revenge...

Dirk got into a fight with a lady at The News Stand in Quaker Square in Akron. Dirk had made a comment about Denise Levertov, which had displeased her, because, as it turned out, she was Denise Levertov. In short, though reports of this incident have been exaggerated somewhat, Levertov hit Stratton with her purse, which was quite heavy, having in it a hardbound copy of *Moby Dick* (a copy that Levertov later was accused of trying to steal from this bookstore), and Stratton, a feminist convinced of the equality and even the superiority of women, punched Levertov in the jaw as hard as he could. Levertov was unfazed by this and the elderly poet threw Stratton up against the Gay and Lesbian Studies shelves, which were knocked over. Both were uninjured and, eventually, even signed one another's books, as police looked on, waiting to take Levertov into custody.

Sometimes when I am lying there, awake, fixated on the corpses of foreign wars, I hear the nearby church chiming three in the still of the icy night, and through the window I can see clouds rushing across a universe of unsurpassable beauty and mystery.

Then I think of disc golf.

Disc golf is not so much a sport as it is an art: flight.

Oh sure, to you, disc golf may seem trivial, mundane, silly, but I assure you that it is in every way a sport whose degree of pro-fessionalism rivals that of even, say, racquetball. No, disc golf is no mere variation of darts for outdoorsmen. Though to believe that America has a sophisticated disc golf community, composed of athletically-minded people (as well as a few errant stoners), you'd have to see the disc golf courses in Cincinnati. No mere walk in the park, these courses are like hiking trails with baskets. This, my friends, is disc golf in the woods.

Scott and Dirk introduced me to disc golf at Mount Airy Forest. *A day at the park is good for a man's constitution.*

And this is when I met Louis, who had played every course. Louis had inhaled mosquitoes rescuing his putters from the teeth of al-ligators in the Florida Everglades. He had endured dysentery on long disc golf expeditions in war-torn Kashmir. He had retrieved his putter from between the long, pointed, razorous spikes of cacti in Death Valley. He had wrestled an octopus at a coral reef in the Galapagos, to reclaim his driver from its tentacles.

When there came a break in our touring schedule, Louis caught up with us in Vegas, and we boarded his Lear jet to Hawaii. There was a disc golf course in Kanai, Louis said: Circle Park. One of the most beautiful—and brutal—disc golf courses in the Western hemisphere.

After landing in the Hawaiian islands, jet-lagged, we checked in to our bungalow, unpacked our drugs, and wound down with Mai Tais poolside, arguing about Guy de Maupassant until we had smoked all of Dirk's Te-Amos.

An hour before dawn, after a restive four hour nap, we breakfasted on coconut milk, espresso, and Hawaiian cigarettes, and took off for Circle Park, tearing through the winding mountain roads in a rented Ferrari. The morning was oddly warm and fragrant, expectant.

We wondered what paradise would demand of us.

Proper footwear is essential, as is a complete collection of discs.

Louis brought the car to a sudden halt. We climbed out, checked our disc bags to make sure our discs were in order. Into our backpacks we stuffed kneepads, mining helmets, coils of ropes. Gear assembled, we set off toward the first hole, all of us silent soldiers walking into battle.

The ringing of distant chains as discs collided with baskets and the shouts of young people floated to us through the bamboo and palms.

We were walking up a narrow ravine toward a rushing of water.

We came upon a vista, and Louis put out his arms to stop us from walking over the cliff. The blue sky and ocean were stunning, surrounding us, and a distant whale blew a plume.

It was time to play disc golf with Louis. In Kanai.

And it was time to tee off.

On the first hole, the basket was set in a cavern behind a waterfall, about fifteen feet in. From the tee, set atop a gigantic boulder, it was necessary to throw your disc through the waterfall, then climb through the water, over wet jagged slippery rocks, to retrieve it.

The danger in teeing off, of course, was of throwing the disc without enough force to penetrate the waterfall, because then your disc would be swept down to the rocks below, and might go downstream for miles before it came to rest, giving you a chance to begin throwing it back upriver.

The par was a generous (by Hawaiian standards): 4. Louis used a powerful overhand vertical tomahawk throw to split the water, and we could hear chains ringing from behind the waterfall even over the rush of the current.

Dirk, and then Scott, threw their discs through the water.

I stood on the rocks and stared at the waterfall, Stingray in hand.

Every throw has a curve; throw a curve.

My disc went through the water. I slipped trying to climb the wet rocks and cut my leg. I finally passed through the waterfall into a cavern lit by a shimmer of refracted light. Inside the cave were stalactites that were difficult to throw around.

Louis, having scored a hole-in-one, was leaning by the waterfall, rolling a stick. After the three Unknown fought to get their discs between the natural formations and into the basket, we left the waterfall and climbed to the next hole.

The trail ended at the lip of a jagged gorge. We parted some vines and on the other side of the crevasse, about ten feet over and ten feet down, was a narrow ledge with a wooden bench and basket.

The crevasse was very deep: a volcanic rift from which hot vapors rose. The bottom was distant and invisible, shrouded in shadowy mist. It was necessary to tee off by throwing down to the ledge. If your first throw missed the ledge, or bounced into the rift, your only option was to throw another disc, and keep trying until you emptied your disc bag. (Most of the holes at Circle Park have, in addition to a par number, a number for failure: a score you are given if you fail to complete the hole, whether due to a lost disc, exhaustion, failure of nerve, death or dismemberment.)

Louis teed off first. He threw a spinner, and the gyroscopic forces held it as it slowly floated across the ravine. But the disc bounced off the edge of the basket, and hit the bench, where the buzzsaw force of his throw split the wood causing the disc to become lodged in a plank.

Louis, disappointed at having already destroyed his chance to score an 18 for the round, shrugged, and then grabbed a handful of vines and swung across the narrow ravine.

We stared after him not really believing that this was happening. We all considered ourselves exceptionally practiced disc golf players, but we were not necessarily ready to swing on vines across a bottomless chasm.

But we did.

Scott lost six discs, Dirk two. I lost eight.

After two holes at Circle Park, I wanted to call it a day. I wanted to cry, to go to the Circle Park Lounge and have Hawaiian liqueurs served out of flaming coconuts and wooden glasses shaped like Easter Island statues. I wanted to go back to Louis' rental car and take off my boots. I wanted to go back to the hotel, have them send up to the suite a round of roast beef sandwiches with pineapple slices and a case of Kirin, and watch ESPN.

But there was more disc golf to be played.

"Shit," Louis muttered, "See those guys?"

"What?" I asked.

"Over there." Louis pointed at a pair down the trail in front of us. "Those guys aren't disc golfers, they're narcs."

There were two smiling older men dressed "casually," with short hair, sneakers, white socks and florid floral shirts tucked into running shorts. One of the men was short and fat with a red shirt, the other tall and thin in a blue shirt. Red shirt threw his disc. Red and Blue shirt both laughed, then walked to pick it up. They glanced at us. They glanced away. Then Blue shirt picked up Red shirt's disc, and threw it back the other way.

A smirk of incredulity crept across Dirk's face: "Where are they going? There's no basket over there."

"These guys always fuck with me," Louis said.

The two men, we quickly realized, were pretending to play disc golf. One of them had a disc bag, the other a visor, but except for these realistic touches, they showed no apparent interest in throwing at the baskets.

"Huh?" Dirk asked. "These guys follow you when you come to Kanai?"

"No, man, always—like, fuckin' everywhere and every minute. They're like my personal narcs. Fuckin' follow me everywhere. Fuckin' assholes."

We looked at each other nervously. No one who knew Louis could be unaware of his fondness for vacationing and associated recreational activities, but two narcs assigned exclusively to him?

With Louis, one never knew, but none of us had any desire to confirm Louis' assertion; for obvious reasons, narcs made the Unknown nervous.

So did Louis, though, when he got agitated.

"And I was looking forward to a peaceful game of disc with you guys, those fucking bastards," Louis hissed, pulling a gun out of the back of his jeans, grimacing and waving it at the narcs as if fanning flies off shit.

"Uh, Louis, hey, man, take it easy. What's with the gun, anyway?"

"Smith & Wesson Model 6904, 12 rounds in a clip, and one more in the chamber, total of 13."

"Isn't it, like, bad luck to have 13 rounds?"

"Dunno. I've never had to use all 13," Louis said.

We were at the tee and I was hoping Louis would put his piece away and impress us with his throwing instead.

This hole was a modest par 2002, and involved nothing short of climbing a mountain peak. Scott stared up at it, nervously weighing his disc in his hand. We teed off.

The first couple of dozen uphill throws were almost fun. An hour later, with one hand I was clinging to the boulder I was perched on, with the other tossing the disc a few feet above me, hoping it would rest on the rock and not slide back down.

I wondered whether we would ever get a chance to eat.

Eventually, the acclivity became extreme. We had reached an asymptote. The mountain was so steep that it became inadvisable to release the disc while throwing. Hanging from rock above a drop I dared not look at, rather than throw, I would reach overhead and wedge the disc carefully into a crack in the stone, before advancing another few feet, following Louis' choice of handholds and footholds, repeating the overhead wedge maneuver, over and over, gasping out my stroke-count between clenched teeth.

But with daylight waning, we finally heard the sound of our discs hitting chains.

We set up camp on the peak and spent the night there, drinking armagnac and listening to Louis tell stories.

As we sweated around our small campfire on the Hawaiian mountain peak, Louis talked about his adventures disc golfing Antarctica. He and his crew had made it there by hitching a ride on a freighter out of Tierra del Fuego. It was a harsh course. Boats could only approach the region at the height of the Antarctic summer when the icebergs were broken up. Louis told us of freezing nights under electric skies, frostbite, and sled dogs that would go mad from the barrenness and need to be shot. Compasses would do strange things. Discs would freeze to gloves. In their trek across the glaciers there was the constant danger of breaking through the ice into the freezing water beneath. Discs would get lost, slicing into the snow so deeply that even the radio trackers didn't work. They carried pickaxes to excavate the baskets from the ice that had buried them, sometimes working for days just to make that final putt. The penguins, he said, would flock to his thrown disc, believing it to be food, and would need to be chased away. And at night, when it was dark and clear, the blazing cosmos laid out above, he saw some very strange things he wasn't comfortable explaining.

"Discs spin the opposite way down there," Louis said, gesturing with his flask as if toasting the night.

"No way."

"It's true. Coriolis forces."

"You're fucking with us, Louis."

The next morning, we awoke on the mountain, very stiff. Down the slope I could see that the plainclothes policemen with red and blue floral shirts were ascending after us.

"Fuckers," Louis said, bringing from his disc bag a shining serrated buzzsaw blade, and sighting along it toward the men below.

"Are they following us?" I asked. "Should we offer to let them play through?"

"Fuck it," Louis said. "Let's just get going."

We never knew the whole story about Louis. He had connections. We knew that he had done some work for a consulting firm interested in building disc golf courses on the moon—some entertainment visionaries or something more sinister. What with the extremely low gravity and lack of atmosphere, it was not clear whether discs would fly straight, tumble end over end or maybe achieve escape velocity and leave the moon altogether. What was clear was that they could be thrown extremely far, and that an 18-hole course might take considerable time to play. Louis had been to the moon as their tester, and some of his drivers were still in orbit.

My jeans were shredded from climbing through the volcanic rock. I took Louis' hunting knife and hacked away their ragged legs, fashioning crude cut-offs. We teed off from the peak, aiming for a crater about a thousand yards away and many hundreds of yards below us.

The wind was brisk and kept changing direction. Louis held out his disc, sighting along his arm toward the distant crater. Then, unexpectedly, he whirled around and threw in the opposite direction. We thought he had gone mad, but the wind took the disc head on and lifted it up and up, well over our heads, and into the sky and behind us. "Left, left!" Louis shouted, spinning, though we weren't sure which left he meant as the disc descended toward the hole, gliding in like a hawk on target.

It was in the air for nearly a minute, until it was a tiny speck of tie-dyed coloration against the mountainside. It hit an up-draft and we watched it climb the mountain for awhile. "Hot spring down there," Louis explained, "creates an updraft that can help you play this hole."

It took us most of the day to find our discs.

Louis' disc had gone into the crater, he presumed, and he sat on a boulder there, with his portable typewriter on his lap, reworking a short story, until we three Unknown each appeared, preceded by our flying discs.

We divided up our last candy bar and descended into the crater, tossing discs before us.

There was no sign of Louis' disc. I was sure it had never made it into the crater, but he was perfectly confident.

We went on through caves, tunneling downward through blackness. At one point, we had to duck to avoid brushing the bats clustered on the cavern ceiling. I followed carefully behind Dirk, the lamp on my helmet casting strange lurching shadows as I scanned the damp grey clay for the bright plastic yellow or red or blue of my disc.

Finally, the passage narrowed to where we had to crawl to get through. We came out in a vast underground cavern whose walls were patterned with luminescent moss. There was a dampness to the air, and the sound of trickling water echoed from the high pointed ceiling. As our eyes made things out, we saw a river, in whose clear depths strange pale fish moved sluggishly. And there, on the other side of the underground river, lit by the play of our flashlight beams reflecting off the water, was the basket.

In which sat Louis' disc.

"I threw a roller," Louis explained.

Compared to the other holes at Circle Park, the holes that hid their baskets behind combinations of mineral and smoke, fluid and flora, light and mirrors, Hole 5 seemed as simple and direct as a bowling lane. The basket was perched on the edge of a cliff at the end of an long and narrow passage created by two parallel rows of immense palm trees.

"What are you throwing on this hole, Louis?" Scott asked, looking forlornly at the severely depleted disc supply in his shoulderbag.

Louis ignored the question. "Do any of you even recognize just how diabolical this hole truly is?"

"Looks pretty straightforward to me," William said.

"It's an optical illusion," said Louis. "These rows aren't really parallel. It's just like it looks: the closer you get to the basket, the closer together the trees get. At the point where a disc can finally get past the last two trees, things are so tight it's like throwing your disc through a vertical mail slot. A good tomahawk isn't sufficient: it's got to be near fuckin' perfect. Either that or you have to hizer your disc somehow, severely, and at exactly the right moment to slip between that final pair of palms. Or you have to lay-up in front of the mail slot and then just stick it through. How lame is that? And then, the friggin' basket is, like, 100 feet beyond the trees next to a cliff overlooking a violent surf that pounds the rocks below. Fuckin' ridiculous. I've never thrown this hole, not once. Never will, either."

Louis began heading for the 6th tee. We continued to look down the palm tree tunnel in an attempt to verify Louis's description.

The sky, I noticed, was made of bricks.

"Hey," Louis said, "if you want to play it, you know, fine. But I'm taking the par. Meet ya on 6."

Taking the par? How does one take the par? Without throwing a disc?

"Perhaps he's become some sort of a black belt Zen priest of disc golf," William offered.

"What's the sound of an unthrown disc striking chains?" Dirk replied solemnly.

"Wow," Scott said. "A disc golf koan."

William teed off. The disc bounced off the first tree and hit him in the head.

They found Louis hanging out at the tee for Hole 6, rolling a limb. This hole was on a vast stretch of beach, on the north side of the island where the waves were as fierce as anywhere in Hawaii. It was nine hundred feet from the tee to the basket, as the seagull flies, but with every throw you were gambling with your disc. At high tide the basket was completely submerged, so the hole could only really be played during low tide, and even then gigantic breakers would push hundreds of yards up the shore. You had to wait for a break between waves, run down to the tee, throw, then run and retrieve your disc before a wave hit it and swept it away in the foaming undertow. And if you reached your disc, you might be staring down a tidal wave many times your height, with nothing to do but stupidly try to cling to a square of sand when it came down upon you. If you were swept away, and managed to hold on to your disc, and did not drown, you might be pushed so far up the beach that you were further from the basket than when you teed off.

And it was there, at Hole 6, that we last saw Louis.

We watched as he took aim at a basket so far way it was just a gleam flickering amidst glittering surf and the white specks of seagulls. And as he prepared to release his monogrammed, custom-made Cyclone with the tie-dye color scheme, we heard him mutter something under his breath that revealed his intentions.

"Hole-in-one."

He ran a few steps, leapt in the air spinning, grunted for emphasis, and executed his finest arc of the day.

The disc sailed into the sky.

The roaring of the surf became quieter, and I noticed a large wave was coming. I squinted at the sea. A very large wave was coming.

The purple dot of the disc descended toward the glint of the basket, and a scatter of gulls rose from the spot, but we could not see whether the disc went in nor hear the chains above the tides. Louis began sprinting toward it. Regardless of whether it had gone in, the disc had to be near the basket, Louis was "there," as we liked to say, it was a gimme putt, for sure, definitely a deuce. The trick would be getting to it before the waves.

Louis ran away from us. As he got smaller, the approaching wave got bigger. It was skyscraper-sized.

"Louis! Give it up!" we shouted.

He raced away. Twenty seconds later we could just see him by the basket. He was doing something. He went to the basket. Was it a hole-in-one?

The wave hit us first. We disappeared into a chaos of turbulent saltwater, but, luckily, the wave pushed us up the beach, and did not drag us out to sea in its dangerous, ravenously thirsty undertow.

When I climbed to my knees in the wet sand, I had lost my backpack, my discs, and, somehow, one of my boots.

Dirk and Scott were within sight, fifty yards down the beach, staggering to their feet.

But there was no Louis anywhere.

We walked around shouting Louis' name until it was dark. Then we sat on the hood of the car and wondered what to do.

The Unknown FBI Files: Summary of Findings
Released through the Freedom of Information Act

It had been reported to our agency through an informant that a writing group known as "Unknown" were engaged in subversive activity, meant to undermine the American literary establishment. Agents of the FBI, in cooperation with members of the MLA, undertook a two-year operation designed to infiltrate and expose their operation.

It is in the interests of America that fiction writers continue to write in a style emulating John Updike, producing "kitchen sink" fiction in which Americans are revealed to have drinking problems, and to speak in meaningless, clipped phrases.

The Unknown, as our investigation revealed, do indeed have a drinking problem, but their tendency to write unrealistic dialogue in which fictional characters speak, and indeed seem to experience the world in complete sentences, appears to compose a serious threat. This fact was of great concern to the participating agencies, particularly the MLA, in whose interests it is to maintain the dominance of fiction critics over fiction writers in academic discourse.

Indeed, one of the things that marks these writers is their intolerance for critics. They despise critics. Not theorists, whom they admire deeply, but the sort of writer who makes their mark doing hack work for online encyclopedias or writing smug book reviews. Like "parasitic fish clinging to the flanks of whales" (quoth Rettberg), critics write irritating ripostes to elaborate works, and thus hope to see their name in print (or, more likely) on the monitor close to the names of those artists they secretly admire, and thus trash, in 1000 words or less and, paid a measely pittance, they then consider themselves "professional" writers. The Unknown made their way the hard way: by making the art they believed in whether or not anybody would publish it or pay them, and their resentment toward those who rode their coattails by pointing out the obvious fact that writers producing their own work at their own expense lacked some of the amenities (such as paid proofreaders) that spoiled professional authors took for granted. As Gillespie wrote in private correspondence to Stratton: "Give them a sophisticated graphical interface, and they bemoan the death of text. Give them good writing, and suddenly they want it to do fucking hat tricks when you move your mouse over it." While such a hatred of reviewers is not unusual on the surface, the devil is in the details.

Following are the results of our investigation.

William Gillespie

William Gillespie, as our investigation concluded, poses no serious threat to American letters.

Gillespie's low general morals, however, are without question. Seven national hotel chains have put Gillespie on their central blacklists for numerous infractions, notably the combustion and inhalation of tobacco in rooms designated as "non-smoking." In-room audio surveillance files have captured audio of Gillespie saying, "Smoking in a non-smoking room is like marrying a virgin."

There is also abundant evidence that Gillespie is overly fond of a group of subversive French writers known as the OooooLaLaPoop [translation uncertain]. Aside from Lafayette, it is well known that the French, despite their putative status as our allies, are in fact desperately opposed to virtually everything we cherish as Americans. Their writers are no exception to this rule. Besides, they write in a foreign language which makes it difficult for us to understand what they're up to. This concerns us. Tentative translations of some of this OooooLaLaPoop-style writing proved to be so unintelligible, we are convinced some complicated code or cipher is probably being used. Still, we can't imagine they pose a threat given that the French rarely bathe, thus making a sneak attack unlikely.

Scott Rettberg

Scott Rettberg, to the best of our knowledge, refuses to admit doubt and seldom speaks in indirect terms. Suspected to be behind several assasination plots, national and international. There are three known contracts out on his life including one put out by operatives of the National Rifle Association, Mothers Against Textual Pornography, and followers of his co-author, Dirk Stratton, including the late actors Martin Sheen and Daniel Day Lewis. An expert at propagating misinformation, Mr. Rettberg wears a variety of disguises and is not deft physically. The subject is reportedly quite clumsy, and has suffered a string of comical if not serious head injuries, nonetheless he is still prone to spin puns, many of which are not at all humorous. Not much of a threat to American letters, this one.

Still, surveillance and phone taps should be maintained for the time being. The possibility remains that Rettberg has merely been purposely playing the buffoon to throw us off the scent.

Dirk Stratton

Dirk Stratton, finally, may be a serious threat to the state of American poetry, and it is our conclusion that he should be eliminated. We have been succesful in blocking him from getting a professional job, but he continues to write sparse Zen poetry, the sheer intensity of which may possibly unseat the dominant paradigm of American poetry, instituted by this agency in the late 1940s.

It is not the purpose of this report to detail the conclusions regarding Stratton: the problem has been transfered to a different agency which it is also not the purpose of this report to name. Regardless. As long as the lines of Stratton continue to be read by professional poetry scholars at a university level, our control over academic American poetry remains compromised.

Date: Tuesday, September 12, 2000, 4:08 PM
From: The Unknown List
To: The Unknown List
Subject: I hope you're not changing too much in 'The Unknown'?

Frank,

We think we've figured a program for you with benefits. Right now you are part-owner of the Unknown with a total of fifty shares. Without membership on the board, however, you are powerless to make any decisions. Now what we're proposing is a slow phase out with a gradual recompensation in character placement options. Meaning that, for each share you sell, your name will replace either Scott's, Dirk's, or my own. This isn't the only option although I suggest you discuss it with your broker. See, we're streamlining and downsizing. We want the whole Unknown to be a slim volume, we're gonna whittle it down to like, 20 pages. An easy read. And we're taking out the links because we're tired of being typecast as "hypertext." See what I'm saying? Now we appreciate the fact that you're on the list and it's great that every couple of months you check your email and toss off a response or an aphorism or epigram or a whit of wisdom—even though you're from Frisco so all your babbling about "energy" and "crystals" doesn't really cut the mustard the way a nice Wrigley Field hot dog would—your hot tub just doesn't hold water, pal, but go ahead and be a golden boy: we don't have as much sex as you and the sun doesn't come out every day in the midwest. No sir, this summer every day the temperature has been between 50 and 110 without missing a beat, so we don't know what it's all about kissing on Golden Gate Bridge when your mouth still tastes like garlic from the like 20, 30 amazing restaurants you went to that day alone. Free love? Sorry, man, we're up to our elbows in our own mystique and we're actually very conservative here in the heartland. You know we're jealous, but we can't ride each other's coattails forever. Sorry you couldn't make it to Chicago for our reading and sorry you couldn't manage to toss off a newspoem while you were writing 10-page fluff pieces for the big paper out there, I forget the name. Yeah, you're all laid and successful and we keep struggling, keep touring, keep giving interviews. How many times have I woken up with a hangover next to Rettberg in a hotel room that smelled like an ashtray all so we could break ourselves promoting your famous novel? I'll tell you: 1,234 times on the nose, man. Well, we've all got our hangups I suppose. So next time you're all messed up on X and Thai sticks groping some teenager in a midnight warehouse while the decibels crank out enough synthetic beat to bring down a 747, just thinking to yourself "the world is my orange," just be glad, man, be glad, because paradise is full of palm trees and one of them just might drop a coconut on you someday. Mark my words. In the meantime, well, just keep writing weird messages and scaring off the European scholars who have climbed to the mountaintop to take counsel with us: the Unknown. We never wanted to be the subject of someone's dissertation, and we sure don't want to go to Europe.

Yeah, right.

Good luck to you.

The Unknown

They had made a bunch of changes to *The Unknown* without asking him. Frank was bitter. He would write them an angry letter as irked coauthor, then he would get on his motorcycle and drive straight east out of San Francisco to catch up with their fictional characters and get them into trouble, into fights with bikers and booksellers. They didn't get it. He was Frank and he was "Frank," and his writing belonged on the red-purple line or maybe the purple-red line. Fuck it, the blue-green line.

How can the fiction and metafiction be at the same diegetic level? Doesn't that render the concept silly beyond tedium? The concept is no longer recursive if its levels are not strictly differentiated. If "William" goes disc golfing in Hawaii, and the photos are all of Illinois, then which is lying? (Photos don't lie, only their contexts lie.) To hell with them, I'm the only one who's real: I'm "Frank." They made me up so I could be their friend, but I'm a lie. Let me be frank: my name is merely an adjective. My prose is a wash of color to fill the void I left. Forgive me if I am forthright, but that is my name. Direct, honest, unflinching, and a lie.

I am frankly art, artifice, artificial. Fill my mold with sorrow. After William is done fixing *The Unknown* he feels like shit and goes home to discover his phone has been disconnected. He didn't open the envelope. What envelope? Will Frank be pissed at him? How should I know? I'm Frank itself. I'm the ultimate chiaroscuro coloratura trompe-l'oiel fin-de-siecle fictional gift. Use me, gentlemen, and build something more useful but less underrated than *Underworld*. If you tell the world that I am frank, they will get the joke, and we will all drown in applause and flashbulbs. But we are no Vonnegut, no Sorrentino, no Gaddis. We take no risks. Our use of ourselves as artifices comes naturally to us. We write poetry about writing poetry and stories about fiction writers and don't even notice a contradiction. It's all one big diegetic level to us, there is no story or narrative other than the staggeringly huge and detailed network of everything thought, written, bragged, denied, or implied: language. No fact and fiction, only the text. We are over metafiction, it is a split hair. It is all fiction, usually wrought by impatient storytellers.

Frankly, my dear, I don't give a damn.

Gaddis wanted to play pool against all three of us. He said he already had his team, that they were all lounging around up there in his head.

Gaddis and Dirk lagged for the break. It was midafternoon and we were the only people in the place. Gaddis won, the cue ball coming to rest the width of a cigarette from the bumper. Gaddis pulled a cigarette from a silver cigarette case he withdrew from the inside pocket of his tweed jacket, offering us each one.

Gaddis lit his cigarette and leaned over the table and broke with one solid stroke, a crack and a technicolor explosion of balls. The two ball went in. Scott went away and came back carrying four pint glasses of Bass Ale.

Gaddis picked up his cigarette and used it and set it down and tried to hit the fourteen ball into the three ball knocking the three ball into a side pocket, but his measured stroke, while accurate, was slightly too gentle and the three ball came to rest beside the pocket. The bartender lit a cigarette and stared through the neon out at the afternoon street and the traffic.

Dirk took the cue, cigarette dangling from lip, and tried to hit the fourteen ball into the side pocket by easing it between the pocket and the three ball; he instead knocked the fourteen ball into the three ball and knocked the three ball in. Gaddis took a long drink and half of his beer was gone; Scott and I each had drunk about an inch and Dirk's was untouched. Gaddis circled the table and told us that the World Wide Web was going to mean the end of literature. That made us feel kind of self-conscious. The bartender collected our empties and replaced our ashtray with a clean one. Gaddis handed him a five as a tip. The bartender said thanks Bill.

Gaddis hit the one ball off two bumpers and into the corner pocket. The cue ball then collided with the eight ball which rolled over to rest within six inches of another corner pocket. The bartender was behind the bar, leaning over and washing glasses.

Gaddis bounced the seven ball off of a side bumper and it came very close to the side pocket opposite. Gaddis put down his cue and finished his beer. I took our cue from Dirk. The bartender turned on the TV It was a rerun of *Seinfeld*. Gaddis murmured bullshit. The bartender turned the TV back off.

I scratched but we hadn't struck in a ball yet so there was none to take back out. Gaddis signaled to the bartender, who nodded and set three shot glasses out and went to find some bottle. Gaddis picked up his cigarette and used it and set it back down again, and took his cue, and set the cue ball on the table.

Gaddis knocked the cue ball down along the side bumper, nearly parallel to it, grazing the seven ball, causing it to roll ever so slightly and fall into the side pocket, and the cue ball then met the four ball and sent it into the corner pocket at the opposite end.

Gaddis then knocked the five ball off three bumpers, missing the pocket, perhaps out of pity.

The bartender came over with three shots, each full to the edge of the glass. I looked and on the bar he had set out a bottle of Johnny Walker Black Label: Gaddis's poison. We lifted our glasses and said nothing and drank. Scott coughed and picked up our cue and put chalk on the tip and rubbed talcum powder on his hands.

Scott leaned over the table and accidentally knocked in the eight ball, losing the game.

Subject: monstrosities
Date: Wed, 29 Mar 2000 10:20:19 -0600
From: William Gillespie <william@wordwork.org>
Organization: Spineless Books
To: Thomas LeClair

Frankenstein's creation is monstrous precisely because it is an artifice assembled from human parts. *The Unknown* is a dismembered four-way auto/biography—with prosthetic appendages. The mixture of authentic personal correspondence and hallucinatory fiction is made all the more haunting by a floating authorship— sometimes an individual, always a subset of the group. Does this thing have a consciousness? Or many?

Monstrous because parts of it are real, even touching, yet the whole is horribly disgusting, bringing into question that reality we had assumed was bearable.

The Unknown looms in the doorway of serious literature, grunting and drooling and fondling itself. The writers, smoking cigars around the card table, pretend to ignore it. It is their prodigal son and they will under no circumstances invite it in.

The Unknown has Julio Cortazar's left arm, Adrienne Rich's heart, Nelson Algren's mouth, Mary Shelley's appendix, Jack Kerouac's liver, Sigmund Freud's colon, and Krass-Mueller's left tennis shoe.

The Unknown tells the story of how King Kong, ruined by the excesses of his own notoriety, became a fallen man; how Elvis Presley became a sort of monster.

Without using the word "cyborg," *The Unknown* is part machine, part human; an electronic book. A malfunctioning robot spills its drink in its lap, shooting sparks.

The Unknown is Undead: a winged, bloodsucking parasite. It is electronic and cannot be destroyed.

The Unknown is that sound you hear downstairs precisely when you are supposed to be asleep and dreaming of the canon.

belch

Dirk's powers were well manifest in Dublin. Most eerie was the resemblance between what Cuchulainn went through during his warp spasms, and how Dirk describes the most frightful of his psychic journeys into the unknown territory of telepathic supernatural investigations. And I don't just mean mushrooms.

Dirk puts it like this:

When the first vision hits me, it's an out-of-body jolt, wham! right away. It seizes me and I see myself, and I am different. It makes me into a monstrous thing, hideous and shapeless, unheard of. My shanks and joints, every knuckle and angle and organ from head to foot, shakes like a tree or a reed in the stream. My body makes a furious twist inside my skin, so that my feet and shins and knees switch from the rear and my heels and calves switch to the front. On my head, the temple-sinews stretch to the nape of my neck, a mighty, measureless knob as big as the head of a month-old child. My face and features become a red bowl: I suck in one eye so deep into my head that a wild crane couldn't peck it onto my cheek out of the depths of my skull; the other eye falls along my cheek. My mouth is weirdly distorted: my cheeks peel back from my jaws until my gullet shows, my lung and liver flapping in my mouth and throat, my lower jaw strikes the upper a lion-killing blow, and fiery flakes large as a ram's ass reach my mouth from my throat. My heart booms loud in my breast like the baying of a dog at its feed or the sound of a lion among lambs. Malignant mists and arcs of fire flicker red in the vaporous clouds that rise boiling above my head. The hair of my head twists like the tangle of a thornbush stuck in a gap, then rises up from the dead center of my skull a straight spout of black blood darkly and magically smoking like the smoke from the Vatican when a new Pope is anointed.

Sure you guys are jealous of my psychic powers, my luck with women, the oversized size of my fan population. But you would not want to be in my shoes. Trust me.

"I am a Palestinian!" declared Dirk, raising his left hand toward the barbed wire.

"But I am also a Jew!" he announced, raising his right hand toward the stretchers being carried out of the smoking ruins of the bus and loaded into ambulances. A soldier waved his machine gun at Dirk, indicating that the three unknown tourists should move on. A squadron of fighter planes screamed overhead.

"Ah-ah," Dirk shook his finger and smiled at the soldier, who did not speak English. "Israel has a law against extraditing Messiahs."

"C'mon, Dirk, let's go," said Scott, nervously tugging at the sleeve of Dirk's robe.

Dirk pulled away. "I am a Shiite!" Dirk cried, gesturing in the general direction of Mecca, "and yet I am also a Sunni!" The mention of these words made the soldier frown and he raised his machine gun. Dirk winked at the guard, and said, "But I am also a Jew!" The soldier muttered something into his radio, not lowering his machine gun nor taking his eyes off the shorn Dirk with the flowing white robes and the golden hoop earring.

"And yet I am also a Nazi!" cried Dirk.

Scott started sweating, and fumbled a cigarette out and lit it, offering one to the soldier, who waved it away and gestured that they should move on. William stared across the barbed wire at the Gaza Strip.

"C'mon Dirk," said Scott, "let's get out of here. Maybe a few days in a Kibbutz will mellow you out."

"I have a hydrogen bomb!" declared Dirk triumphantly, raising both hands to the sky. Another soldier arrived, gun at the ready.

William started to walk slowly away, trying his best to look Orthodox. A third soldier stopped him.

The second soldier scrutinized Dirk, squinting, then his eyes brightened. "Unknown!" he said. Then repeated it in Hebrew for the benefit of the first soldier, who shrugged.

"I am a poet! And yet I am also a hypertext novelist!"

The first lawsuit we barely felt. It was like a gnatbite. Didn't break the skin.

Then the Microsoft suit came as kind of a slap in the face, but then at that point we still had careers to be ruined.

When we got subpoenaed by Melville we were taken aback. The man was dead and his work was public domain, but these were mere technicalities in the face of an accomplished litigator. Well, we told them to fuck off since our website had already been taken down, our property was gone, we had each been ditched, divorced, or spurned, and we were sure they wouldn't be able to find us where we were hiding in our cave near Kandahar.

Of course we hadn't counted on Allah declaring a class action lawsuit against the surviving members of the literary rock band formerly known as Unknown, so replete with bristling testimonials, exhibit As, filibusters, heart attacks on the witness stand, claims, fees, and funds that we just decided to chuck it. We skipped our court date and descended to hell.

Of course once we had passed beyond the river of the damned into the underworld, we were extremely vulnerable to all kinds of lawsuits from people who were dead, mythical beasts, and even Dante himself for our infringing upon his trademarked afterlife.

They've ruined our lives and fucked our bones, but they can't take away our unknown.

It looked as though Barnes & Noble's antitrust case was going to drag on in courtrooms for years as the corporate giant methodically monopolized the publishing, distribution, and bookselling industries.

And then there was the time when the Unknown came into the Barnes & Noble in Billings, Montana, on Harley Davidson motorcycles. Their choppers rumbled in through the front doors and lined up beside the sale table, idling. The four writers wore helmets with American flags and leather jackets with the URL of the hypertext emblazoned across the back. They began to rev their engines to terrifying volumes, drowning out the Muzak even in the computer books section in the rear corner of the superstore. There were shouts and security officers running toward them from both the café on the right and the long row of cash registers on the left.

Dirk nodded, and the four bikes tore off in different directions. Dirk and Scott drove straight up the middle of the store, literature to their right, history and politics to their left. Customers with shopping baskets yelled and fled into the science fiction and poetry aisles.

Frank pulled a radical wheelie and drove off to the left between the remainder tables. He kicked over a stack of copies of first edition hardcovers of *A Frolic of His Own* marked down to $3. A security guard chasing him tripped over the copies of the great encyclopedic novel and hit the floor in a cloud of unattributed dialogue.

William's great bike circled to the right and tore toward the café, scattering newspapers in its wake. A security guard vaulted the counter of the cafeteria, kicking over a glass jar of overpriced biscotti, which hit the tiled floor in a splash of glass and crumbs. The guard leapt onto a table, stepping on a screaming under-graduate's open copy of *A Room of One's Own*, and dove over the railing of the café onto William's bike as it drove past. The guard grabbed the chrome on the back of William's seat. William gunned the engine and took a hard right around a tight corner, sweeping the guard up and off his feet, and slamming him into a tall shelf of sheet music, where he fell stunned to the blue car-pet. William banked left and noticed a copy of Helene Cixous's *The Ladder of Reading* on the critical theory shelf as his speedometer hit 30 MPH. He was scared but kept telling himself, "This will make a great scene in the movie, this will make a great scene in the movie..."

On the opposite side of the store, Frank was tooling down a narrow row between nature and science books, being chased by a screaming assistant manager, when a very big security guard appeared in front of him at the front end of the aisle. Frank, keeping his hands on the handlebars, leapt up onto the seat, crouching on his boots, gunned the accelerator, and sprang into the air. The bike tore into the guard and drove him into a shelf of travel books, which exploded in a chaos of unfolding maps. Frank sailed over the shelf as it fell apart and, in midair, he grabbed the chandelier, swinging back and forth above the noise and smoke.

While Scott diverted security by doing donuts in the children's books section, scattering tiny furniture and toys, leaving skid-marks on the pink carpet, as children huddled in the corners screaming with laughter, Dirk skidded to a stop beside the an-thology section. Smoke rising from his tailpipe, he unzipped his leather jacket, grabbed all three copies of *The Unknown: An Anthology*, and tucked them away, zipping his jacket back up. He then spoke into his helmet radio the line, "So may every humiliated mouth, teeth like desecrated tombstones, fill with the angels of bread." This was their prearranged signal to leave: it meant that the mission had been accomplished.

Having shoplifted back their own books, they were depriving Barnes & Noble whatever markup they would have made off of them. Security guards leapt aside as Scott tore out of the children's section, a gigantic stuffed Cat-in-the-Hat under his arm.

William and Dirk pulled into the main aisle and they made for the exit.

Frank dropped from the chandelier, landing next to his fallen bike. The assistant manager lunged for him. Frank hit the carpet in a shoulder-roll and somersaulted into reference, bouncing to his feet wielding a hardbound abridged *Oxford English Dictionary*. The assistant manager whirled into a fighting stance, and jumped into a flying kick aimed at Frank's faceplate. Frank ducked beneath the kick and brought the open OED up, slamming it shut on the assistant manager's genitals. The assistant manager fell for the floor, yelling, going for a concealed .33 semiautomatic pistol in an ankle holster.

Frank righted his bike, leapt atop it, and motored down the aisle. There were now mall police on the scene, coming at him from the left and the right. Frank drove straight into a low shelf of business books, knocking it over, and he gunned the bike up it like a ramp, sailing over customers lying on the floor, onto the remainder table, where he executed a turn and headed for the door. A bullet tore through a remaindered copy of Philip Roth's *I Married a Communist*.

Scott, on Dirk's cue, had driven back into the storeroom, following a route on a map he had memorized. He drove between shelves of cartons of books, all marked Ingram, and came out at the edge of the loading dock where Marla, in a black dress with a large hat and a veil, stood, smoking a cigarette on a long ivory stem, a carton under her arm labeled Unknown. During the diversion on the main floor, she had made her way into the storeroom and retrieved all the copies of the *Anthology* in the back.

Scott gave her the stuffed Cat-in-the-Hat.

Marla raised Scott's faceplate, kissed him, and climbed onto the back of the bike, wrapping her arms around him. Then she said, "Scootaloo, baby, or we'll be late for your reading at Moose Rack Books in Big Sky."

Scott gunned the engine and they flew off the edge of the loading dock into the night.

The Unknown were hoping to reach Lincoln, Nebraska by dawn. They had a reading at Lee Booksellers at 8:30 A.M. and were running late, as usual.

William was in one of his unspeakably foul funks in the back seat. He was withdrawn and angry and narcissistic and vicious and had become very drunk but was convinced that it was someone else's fault even though he wouldn't pass the liquor. Dirk and Scott drove on in strained silence, each of them separately considering just throwing William out of the car. Their only consolation was that there was no computer in the car so William couldn't flame them over email. William was eating Cheetos and drinking Goldschlager and not sharing either.

They drove through the beautiful and deep night with the amazingly clear stars wheeling above them. A gigantic moon sat on the western horizon behind them. The three men were words, the highway was a ribbon of blank paper. It was a beautiful night and a hostile silence. They drove on into the Unknown in the awesome night beneath constellations they had only known by name.

Abruptly William began to choke. Scott lit a cigarette. Dirk turned on the radio and tried to find a country station. There was a coughing and a strained gargling and a retching. Scott took a deep drag and looked out the window and said: "I don't know the Heimlich maneuver. Do you?"

"Nah," Dirk replied.

There was nothing to be done. William was gasping, trying to loosen a Cheeto from his trachea.

"If he choked to death," Scott offered, "it would be just like John Bonham."

"That would be cool, actually," agreed Dirk, "if the Unknown could be more like Led Zeppelin. They sold a lot of records."

"Yeah. Also, I think Frank is really getting tired of being compared to Ringo."

There was a prolonged strangled wheeze and a thumping. Dirk asked Scott:

"Didn't Keith Moon choke on his own vomit?"

"Who?"

"Yeah, er, no, not the whole Who, Keith Moon was just the drummer."

"I thought he died by falling out of a second story window."

"No, er, yeah. Well, I mean, he did fall out of a second story window. But he was uninjured."

"That a fact?"

William's arm reached up from behind the front seat and tapped Scott on the shoulder. Scott offered him a cigarette, wondering aloud: "Now wait, how did Jim Morrison die?"

"It was probably a cocaine and alcohol overdose, but I don't think he was ever autopsied. I think he was vacationing overseas with a lover and she was the only witness."

"Ah. Yeah, I remember, but yeah, hmm... And Hendrix?"

"He overdosed on pills. I think it might have been a prescription sleeping pill he was actually taking in order to sleep. Thing was, the ambulance drivers didn't treat him properly, probably because of who he was. I think they just propped him up in the back seat, and he choked to death on the way to the hospital."

"Really. What about Janis Joplin?"

"Heroin and whiskey. Joplin and Hendrix were both 27. It was 1970. Hendrix died in September, Joplin in October. Hendrix in London, Joplin in Hollywood."

"And Morrison?"

"1971. 28, I think."

"And Brian Jones? How old was he when he drowned in a swimming pool in 1969?"

"He was 27, too. But the Rolling Stones had already asked him to leave the band."

"How old is William?"

"I forget."

"Didn't rock stars shoot themselves back then?"

"No. Only writers."

"Shit."

"What?"

"Well, I'm just thinking. All those people were dead by the time they were our age."

"So?"

"So they all had at least, what, three, four albums, a couple TV shows, whatnot. All we got is one stinking measly book and it took three of us to write it."

"Don't remind me. Time's winged chariot. But don't forget the hypertext, the criticism."

"Yeah, all that shit. Didn't any rock stars get shot in the Sixties?"

"No. Only politicians and African-American leaders got shot in the Sixties. Sixties rock stars didn't start getting shot until the Seventies."

"Hey William, you okay?"

"...ugh..."

"Is that a yes?"

"...'sthere any water up there?"

"I don't know. Ask Dirk."

"...Dirk?"

"Yeah, Zeppelin, I don't know. Last I heard, the number one song of all time was "Hey Jude" and "Stairway to Heaven" number two. I think we should stick with the Beatles. Frank always seemed like more of a George Harrison to me. You guys often treat me like Ringo."

"And who's John Lennon?"

"I don't know. Lennon was supposedly really grumpy and withdrawn and arrogant and fucked up a lot of time."

"Hm..."

"He also got murdered by a psychotic fan who had cultivated a cult-leader kind of fixation on the man."

"Hm...I guess I don't know which of us is Lennon."

"Yeah, we'll just have to wait and see..."

"...Dirk...?"

"Well, this is it."

William's jaw dropped. At first all he could see was the skyscrapers before them as seen through the floor-to-ceiling windows of the new Unknown office on the top floor of the Coyote building at the corner of Damen, North, and Milwaukee, across the street from Borderlines and Wicker Park Dogs, in Chicago, a city on the make, a city that worked. Scott smiled. He'd had the entire floor rehabbed—money being no object. And it was a great neighborhood, with that cool Quimby's bookshop with all the zines right down the street. Dirk walked in through the massive walnut doorframe and put a hand to his forehead.

"It's fucking gorgeous!"

Scott nodded: "It suits us, I think."

William stood by the window dazzled by the metropolis, the strength of the buildings rising from the littered asphalt city floor, agog from the sheer velocity of commerce, the taxicabs below tracking their silent vectors through grey streets teeming with pedestrians.

Dirk walked around, his keen eyes taking in the brickwork, the stamped tin ceiling, the color Xerox machine capable of handling 11x17, the thermal binding equipment, the grand oak desks each with a view that would make even a jaded Wall Street investor pee his pants.

He found his desk, which Scott had ornamented with a cloth-bound first edition of *Ark*, and a bottle of Booker's—just like the night this all got started.

Dirk felt something he had never felt before. He thought it might be money.

William was passing boo, smiling (Scott tried to remember if William had ever smiled before), just giddy. Scott slid open a long drawer in his desk and brought out a silver champagne bucket, with a bottle of Moet Chandon White Star resting in half-melted ice, silver tongs tinkling against the side of the bucket. He also brought out three Tiffany champagne flutes and set them on his magisterial blotter beside the framed photograph of Marla wearing her white sun-dress.

William felt something he had never felt before, he thought it might be happiness.

Scott deftly twisted off the wire harness. With a pop, the cork, trailing its foil, blew off the overexcited bottle without coaxing, rapping hard against the triple-paned glass, ricocheting off the track lighting, and spinning to rest in the center of William's desk.

Scott felt something he had never felt before, he had no idea what it was.

It felt good. He poured three foaming glasses and the young writers all lifted them in appreciation of a moment they never thought they'd live.

We had a little reading at Paperback Plus Books in Broken Arrow, Oklahoma and it was kind of depressing. More than 10% of the books there were remaindered, and there were many copies of *A Frolic of One's Own* by William Gaddis. Gaddis was dead, and it was depressing that he was dead. We thought we had played pool with him, but that was only a collective hallucination, that we had had back when he was still alive. Back in 1998. That was such a long time ago. But his books were there, remaindered. There were very few of us there, that had read it. Our reading was complete shite.

We didn't like each other anymore. We had taken advantage of each other in complex ways and scarred each other emotionally. Scott, in pursuit of his dream that he had assumed was ours, which it was not, had compromised us in unforgivable ways. He had stopped writing, as far as we could tell, though we could not. Who can?

I won't belabor the point. There was nothing but Garth Brooks on the radio in Oklahoma. We ate some venison and potatoes there, and told stale jokes about Dan Quayle. The jokes were cruel and unfunny but they were the only ways we could get each other to laugh any more. How sad. Scott told a joke about Bambi that nearly made me ill. This was the state of the Unknown? It was not any longer what it once was.

Used books usually make me happy. Remaindered books always make me sad.

I was sad that there were so many used copies of *The Unknown: An Anthology* there at Paperbacks Plus, but glad that none of them were remaindered. Most of them had their spines cracked, so they were used, but not all the way. By examining the pages, I could tell that some people had only made it to "Grammar Primer," others had stopped on "Laiku," and still others, sadly, never even made it past "The Meddlesome Passenger."

I got mad at Scott, but I didn't say anything to him. He was walking around with a deep, hurt, wounded, remaindered look on his face. I was mad at him for forgetting how much fun writing hypertext was. He assured me that he had stuff in the works. But you could tell that was a lie.

I won't talk about Dirk's bullshit or Frank's whining, or my own back problems. But I will tell you that life is short, too short to be wasting it on the Unknown.

They called the town Broken Arrow, and that has a lot to do with Native Americans. That's how I felt that night too. Once we were an arrow piercing the heart of America. But the arrow was broken, really, broken irreparably.

We ate venison and potatoes, and then found a disc golf course. We played without speaking to each other. It would go on for weeks like that. Little did we know.

So we were released from prison, finally, and we were given back our confiscated possessions—mostly 1500 copies of *The Unknown: An Anthology* and some cassettes. Marla, who had paid our bail in Anchorage with an Illinois Arts Council grant, had lined up some gigs in Seattle.

The drive back through Canada was solemn, meditative; indeed, if we had we observed Dirk more carefully, we might have called it religious. Dirk's head had been shaved while he was in jail, he sat in the lotus position, even while driving, and he spoke little. Our passage to Seattle had the aura of a pilgrimage, and Dirk seemed to regard our jail time not as a nuisance, but as a sort of confessional after which he was now absolved of all sin and part of his critical faculties.

We got across the border without incident.

Dammit, Rettberg, you're telling it all wrong. Those were crazy days and your memory isn't what it used to be. Of course you don't know that because you don't remember when you had a memory. Would you listen to me for a second? I'm eighty-one but I ain't dead and my mind's as clear as a fucking bell, you toothless bastard. My mind is like a mountain pond on a windless day. And I don't need no fucking Viagra. There's plenty of love here at the retirement community. Women and men, we're all well-rested, medicated, mature, and very frisky. But I digress, don't have a fucking heart attack, okay pal? Jiminy. Anyhow, what I want people to remember is the eighties. That's right, the nineteen eighties. When you had your B. Dalton and your Waldenbooks, and that was it. Reagan, you wanna talk about a senile bastard, that motherfucker, don't get me started. I tell you, I'm eighty, but I lived seventy of those years back in 1999. The nineties. Fucking nineties. We lost Bukowski, Zappa, Leary, Rubin, Ginsberg, Burroughs, and Hunter S. Thompson, that loony bastard, died in that motorcycle crash. So there we were with no literature anymore. And what we did was to just put our asses out there and say: "Look at the state we're in, is this the best we can do, America? Can we get some more writers, please?" And they loved us. Or so we thought. Rettberg? Rettberg? Wake up, you insulin-shooting skeleton, these long-distance calls cost more than Depends. Wake up! Scott....?

William stood in the dark beside the pool sadly. The strains of "Tequila" by the Champs drifted through the cool night air. Inside, through the gigantic window, he could see Scott and Dirk dancing with two women wearing haltertops, miniskirts, fishnet stockings and bunny ears. Hugh Hefner, clad in pink silk pajamas and white gloves, was too old and fat to do much more than shuffle, but he clearly was having a good time entertaining the Unknown. Scott was wearing somebody's boxers on his head and everybody was laughing.

William sighed. The guys sure were having a good time. Maybe he should just relax for once, just for one night, what harm could it do...? Then he thought about Naomi Wolf. And Susan Faludi. And Susan Jacoby. And he remembered Susan Brownmiller's phrase: "Pornography is the distilled essence of anti-female propaganda."

Another woman with bunny ears came outside with a tray of martinis and walked up to William to try again to get him to come inside and enjoy the gathering. William reluctantly accepted a martini. He looked at her and asked "what's your name?"

"Bunny."

"No it's not, don't be ridiculous. That's so diminutive."

"I don't mind."

"Besides, isn't there another woman here named Bunny?"

"Yes. We're all named Bunny. My full name is Bunny 12."

William sighed. "Well, do you mind if I call you Catherine A.

MacKinnon?"

"No. That's fine."

"Do you even know who that is?"

"Actually, I studied with her. I have a Ph.D. in women's studies and I'm currently a second-year law student."

"What? What are you doing here?"

"Making two hundred dollars an hour. Do you know how much it costs to take the bar exam? And tuition?"

"Wow. You're much better educated than me! Wait, that sounds insulting, I mean, I thought…Have you read our work?"

"No. When I'm not studying the law, I read critical theory. I don't have time for fiction. Anyway, from what I've heard of *The Unknown*, it sounds kind of silly."

William watched her walk away, then forcibly averted his eyes. Inside the mansion, Dirk was attempting to limbo while wearing a lampshade on his head. The strains of "Wild Thing" by the Troggs floated across the pool. Scott was talking to two women who had their backs turned toward William, who turned away.

It was then that William noticed a man sitting alone on the edge of a fountain across the lawn. William tossed back his martini, set the glass down on the diving board, and walked across the lawn through the darkness and crickets and the smell of freshly-cut grass to introduce himself to the other wallflower.

The man looked up at William and smiled. He appeared to be in his sixties or seventies. He was wearing a suit with the trouser cuffs rolled up. He had big glasses and his hair was disheveled.

William stuck out hi hand: "Hi. I'm deeply offended by all of this. My name is William."

The man laughed and returned the handshake. "Hi William, I'm Noam."

"Gnome?"

"No. Noam. Chomsky."

William stuttered. "Chomsky? *The* Noam Chomsky?"

"Is it a common name?"

"Wow. I'm astonished. You're my favorite—um—dissident. I never thought I'd meet you." William looked around in disbelief at the Playboy estate with its dramatically lit ornamental horticulture and statues of nude women.

"I don't know why I come to these things."

"Why *do* you come to these things."

"Well, I felt I owed it to Hugh. I mean, it's so hard for me to get media attention in America. You know, I go overseas and the major television networks roll out the red carpet for me, I'm very much respected, but here?"

"Yeah. But isn't *Playboy*, like, just as much a tool to manufacture consent as *The New York Times*? I mean, isn't it worse?"

"They won't publish my writing in the *Times*. Or any newspaper or magazine. In America. But Hugh is letting me run a three-parter on this absurd notion of the 'rogue state.' And Kosovo."

"Wow. I, um, am here with the Unknown. Have you heard of us?"

"No."

William excitedly tried to explain to Noam Chomsky *The Unknown*, in all its majesty and scope, from the genesis of the idea in Cincinnati in 1998, all the way through the hypertext novel and the book tour. As he talked about the motion picture he noticed that Chomsky's eyes had glazed over and he was staring at the pool. William trailed off.

After a moment, Chomsky said: "That sounds completely silly. I don't know why I come to these things."

What was unusual was that Robert Pinsky, Poet Laureate, and William did not strike one another with their fists. Instead they decided to have a competition: with two typewriters, a bottle of Booker's, and an ashtray, they were to have a villanelle contest. There was a starting pistol and they both started typing with amazing speed. The crowd in the bookstore went wild. Wagers were placed on who would finish first, whose would scan better, whether there would be slant rhyme, etc. The staff at the bookstore loved us, and they were all jumping up and down in the Critical Theory section, hooting, and cheering Pinsky on. I think Dirk took advantage of the hubbub to steal from the till, but he ended up buying everyone drinks all night, after William won on all counts, most notably for finding rhymes for both "orange" and "silver," and, according to their gentleman's agreement, Pinsky declared William the new Poet Laureate, which honor William promptly awarded to Dirk. Tears were shed.

They wrote it with acid, they wrote it with beer
They wrote it with shrooms and with schwag
They worked on it nightly for nearly a year
They emptied out many a bag.

Come would-be novelists, young poets too
Come here and sit by my side
And listen: I'll tell you a story or two
About four young writers who tried

What the hell? An electronic pastoral novel?
Such a thing: it can never be done!
Such a thing would indeed be much too hard to read
(Such a thing, though, could also be fun)

An experiment, tres avant-garde (to be sure)
Would require some patience to read
And wrought by four stylists unclean and impure
It might get quite raunchy indeed

A poet named Dirk, a writer named Frank
Novelists William and Scott
They all enjoyed working and each of them drank
And geniuses they were all not

They wrote it with acid, they wrote it with beer
They wrote it with shrooms and with schwag
They worked on it nightly for nearly a year
They emptied out many a bag.

Good Scott from Chicago first saw the potential
Of writing an infinite text
With convolutions yet self-referential
So immature, yet so complex

Named after Gaddis, thin William wrote lines
Ten scenes and a chapter or two
Though still there was not any semblance of plot
He still seemed to know what to do

And Dirk from Ohio then took up the thought
And wrote about writing about
He got so recursive that his more discursive
Dear friends had to drag him back out

Meanwhile in Frisco a colleague of theirs
Provided some quite solid text
And then altogether through all kinds of weather
They wrote then they wrote then wrote next

They wrote it with acid, they wrote it with beer
They wrote it with shrooms and with schwag
They worked on it nightly for nearly a year
They emptied out many a bag.

It started one evening like many a curse
It seemed to make sense at the time
And so the whole process was wrought in reverse
So weird it was almost a crime

They began at the end and then worked toward the start
At the onset first one of them died
Then came the movie then Frank's broken heart
And then they got famous and snide

Then penniless, each took a turn at the wheel
And they toured the wide U S of A
They passed through Nebraska, did time in Alaska
And drank shots in Chesapeake Bay

Now working backwards the fun part was done
They were thinner and had much more hair
In order to finish they now had begun
To publish the book. Would they dare?

They wrote it with acid, they wrote it with beer
They wrote it with shrooms and with schwag
They worked on it nightly for nearly a year
They emptied out many a bag.

Ritual of the Unknown

Inhale deeply, and pass the bowl to your left.

The bowl is filled with bitter herbs. The bitterness represents the bitterness of a starving, unpublished writer. The bowl is to remind you of all the suffering your people have endured.

Stand to recite *The Unknown*.

Then recline to the left to drink the wine as befits nobles who once reclined at symposia (intellectual drinking banquets).

If there are no pillows on the chairs, ask the children to bring as many as possible.

Half a muffin, a bunch of coffee, and untold cigarettes. Then: two Bloody Marys on the plane. Then, during the extended Denver layover: first, two pints and three cigarettes. Then, when the flight was further delayed, a 14-oz glass of Avalanche. Then, another pint and another cigarette. Then, on the plane, another Bloody Mary. Then, in the airport, more cigarettes, and then, two margaritas. And a nice dinner. And then three beers.

And the bars have closed.

Will he let me take a shower now, and sleep, for it has been a long day, two, three, four, five days.

And then I look up from the computer and there he is swaying, gin and tonic in hand, and there is a stranger with him, a stranger he has just now met in this town where he knows nobody, and brought to this hotel room.

And they smoke most of the weed, what little weed there is.

And they are telling me to go to a party. A wedding reception down the hall. And I do not want to go. And they are insistent to the point of physically dragging me.

His name is Rusty.

Once I get to the reception, I want to be there even less. There are men in tuxedo shirts who appear at best ambivalent toward me. Large men, from Texas, and women dressed in such a manner that to look at them is to turn them into objects of desire. Their faces are pale and flushed, their expressions stony.

And I want to leave. And Rusty will not let me. And I make

him get me a beer and he does. And then there is a sound going around that we are being expelled from the room and will reconvene in the lobby. In the confusion of people, many many people as this room is a suite of at least two connected rooms, with mirrors, and it is difficult to say just how far this mass of large ambivalent Texans extends, I want nothing more then to get away from them, these strangers celebrating this sacred marriage of two people who have long since left the hotel.

And I escape.

And I am in our room and the crowd is moving down the hallway and then there is Rusty and Scott in the room again. Why did he let him back in here? I want to be alone and sleep. And then Rusty smokes the rest of my weed and I let him because it is my last hope that he will not come back.

But he will not let me stay. He insists that I will go to the lobby with him. In the lobby, I expect, are a mass of people. In this mass of people I stand a good chance of being able to lose Rusty. If I act agreeable, and do not argue, then Rusty will understand that I want to and will party with him, he will be satisfied, his mind will eventually drift on to other things, other people, people he knows, at this wedding he was invited to, and I will be able to leave unnoticed, as well I should, and I will not let him come back into the room, and he and Scott can go on and on and bullshit and drink and party.

Earlier I wasn't able to eat very much, because my food was served on a plate on a corrugated steel tabletop in the numbingly futuristic purple curves of the ostentatious restaurant and as I, the only one eating, tried to eat, I faced, across the table, a semicircle of very serious Norwegian hypertext scholars, who wanted to speak to me about Linguamoos, and I was confounded by their accents, the deafening music, and the fact that my ears had not fully recovered from the flight from Seattle. All of which perfectly ruined my appetite. And then the friends I was with persuaded me to go to a bar. I wanted to sleep, but was able only to voice that desire, not enforce it, perhaps realizing that it was futile, that either I would arrive home late and drunk with these people, or I would be awakened by them later.

In the lobby there are only scattered people. There is a waterfall. There are escalators and a grand piano. There is a spaciousness, a depth, an elegance, a seriousness. Rusty and I go outside where, I think, I can smoke a cigarette, although I do not want one, because I am being forced to mingle among people who do not want me, among whom I truly do not belong, and by smoking a cigarette I can appear practical, natural, no longer at the party but outside, where people who smoke need to be.

I will not be able to escape though. Because I am being buttonholed by a stranger with maniacal eyes, telling me things I do not want to hear.

How does it end? It ends when Rusty does not let Scott into the room. From inside the room I observe through the peephole as Rusty leaps up and down, yelling "Toga! Toga!" and moves, like a basketball player, between my friends and the door to our hotel room, Rusty's back to me in the fisheye lens. Finally they disappear into the elevator, apparently able to get Rusty to go back to his own hotel, by leading him there, manipulating his herd instincts.

In my dreams that night, I hid behind the piano.

I ran up a dead escalator. Rusty was halfway up behind me, moving with incredible speed. But he slipped and rolled to the bottom, which must have hurt. I made a break across the conference room to one of twin staircases moving up. I turned the corner and pressed myself against the wall, breathing hard. I heard nothing. I didn't dare peek around the corner. To my right was a bank of light switches.

I peeked down on the conference room and Rusty looked up and saw me just as I killed the lights.

In the men's room, it starts for Scott as a supernova in the sinuses. Tingling crackles through his opiate fog, igniting his extremities through a nervous system as overworked as a shaky string of Christmas tree lights. He feels his face turn to wood, an antiseptic novacaine, a waterfall of bitter mucous down the back of the throat. Thus he begins a weightless jitterbug on the surface of the ocean, down into which a rusted, barbed net will drag him at dawn.

Dirk had ordered two Bloody Marys and drank both, with two lit cigars in the ashtray before him. For his second round he ordered a buttermilk—tall—and a filet mignon—rare.

Scott returned to the bar and smoked cigarettes through cocaine-dusted stubble, staring sweating at the stocks scrolling by beneath the tennis match on the TV above the bar.

William smoked a special herbal cigarette he swore to the barmaid was not marijuana but was in fact primarily skullcap with sage and a few herbs considered sacred by the Dakota—all legal—which perhaps accounted for its pungent tang.

Scott's eyes went dead. "We're ruined, boys. Game over."

Dirk drained his buttermilk and glanced up at the TV. ASCRAQ, the index of art-related stocks, had dropped fifty points in two seconds.

Scott's cellphone went off. He yanked it from his suit jacket as if it had bitten him. He stared at it in horror. It rang again. He dropped it in his beer. It sparked and went dead, and a bubble of smoke erupted from the foam.

William scratched his head confusedly. "Does that mean that the Unknown isn't as good anymore, or..?"

Scott's pager went off. He threw it to the floor and ground it out beneath a wingtip.

Dirk waved away William's comment. "That's just a statistical index of the value of certain commodities."

Scott climbed off his barstool and stood unsteadily, clawing to loosen his tie. "That's it, then..." he muttered.

Scott picked up his barstool, slung it over his shoulder, and walked toward the window at the edge of the bar on the top floor of the John Hancock Building, the lights of Chicago an incandescent chasm beneath. William moved to restrain him as Dirk's steak arrived steaming from the kitchen.

Dirk ordered a ginger beer, soy milk, and a shot of lab alcohol. And two beers for Scott and William, and, as an afterthought, two more beers for himself.

The view was staggering. Scott threw his stool against the window to shatter it so that he might step out into the cold wind and death beyond, but the stool bounced back off the supersealed glass, ricocheting off his skull, and he slumped to the mahogany-tiled floor unconscious, knocking over a potted fern in an arc of soil.

William surveyed his unconscious collaborator, then returned to drink the two beers Dirk had ordered.

Dirk continued to explain finance to William: " Oh sure, a few big congloms have tried to buy up art, but there just isn't the money to be made there, and, not surprisingly, good artists make bad employees. There's issues about content and production time and demeanor."

"Oh," agreed William. William then leaned close to Dirk and lowered his voice so their unconscious collaborator, snoring loudly beside the dented brass rail, wouldn't hear:

"I'm thinking I might try to cash in on this whole Unknown thing," William explained.

Dirk waved away William's comment, continuing his earlier thought: "You see, it's all speculative. None of that art actually exists yet."

During the final years of their lives, the Unknown wrote exclusively hypertext novels. Many believe that their last hypertext novel contains the Unknown's greatest writing. It represents a culmination of their ideas on lyricism and their experiments with narrative forms. Like their earlier linear works, their final hypertext novel communicates deeply personal, heartfelt sentiments.

The Hypertext Novel in A-flat Major, the Unknown's 31st hypertext novel, was dedicated to Curtis White. While the copyright is dated December 25, 2021, proofreading postponed its completion until a while longer, and the hypertext novel was first posted on servers in Paris, Berlin, and Vienna in 2022. It finally appeared in America in 2023.

The final novel was commissioned by Prince Nikolei Golitsin, a hypertext novel enthusiast from St. Petersburg. He sent email to the Unknown on November 9, 2022, inviting them to compose "one, two, or three hypertext novels" for whatever fee they thought proper. After completing this hypertext novel for the Prince, continued composition in the hypertext medium seemed part of the journey for the Unknown. Given the Prince's enthusiasm and support, it appeared that the Unknown would continue composing in the hypertext medium in perpetuity.

Alas, it was not to be.

The difficulty of their final hypertext novel, described as "700 pages of rhythmic violence and almost ruthless density of thought" by one narratologist, proved to be an insurmountable stumbling block to both readers and critics in the early twenty-first century.

Santa Monica Boulevard, address Unknown. Dirk was dressed as Santa Claus, rolling a joint. A rivulet of blood tickled from his nostril. He was laying out his drugs on an issue of *Rolling Stone*. Scott looked away. William was on the cover of the *Rolling Stone*. It was obvious to Dirk that Scott was jealous, and so Dirk laid out his reds and greens and blues, his ritalin ephedrine ecstasy ibuprofen epiphany, in a mosaic of oval capsules, languorously. Before that, he had been laying down a heavy rap about the Illuminati, about J.R. "Bob" Dobbs. Scott looked out the window. Was this Delaware, Wyoming, Utah, North Carolina, South Dakota? Dirk arranged the STD, LSD, MDT. Dirk is high like Alpha Centauri, low like Lucifer, visionary like Hitler. Dirk had, with his abacus of hallucinogens, uppers, downers, narcotics, tranquilizers, steroids, solved the Kennedy assassination. His nose was bleeding because, hours earlier, he had shattered the mirror he was doing lines off of, and then did an inadequate job of separating the cocaine dust (his last gram) from the glass dust, snorting everything, lacerating his nasal membranes into a bleed that seemed incurable.

But, really, despite all appearances, my aspirations are decidedly modest, Dirk said. I've just been parroting my reading; all the connections were made by others, long before I knew anything. So if this pharmaceutical menagerie provides even the brief illusion of some transcendental vision, I'll be satisfied. The metaphysical equivalent of an overpriced roller coaster ride would be more than sufficient.

Yeah, Scott mumbled bitterly, after all, not everyone can get their picture on the cover of *Rolling Stone*.

William took out his ukulele and started strumming a barely recognizable version of the Dr. Hook song of the same name.

And I keep getting richer, but, William sang.

Fuck, Scott, see, man, that's your problem, Dirk said. Listen, I'd be happy to just have some stupid piece of crap I wrote mentioned in the same magazine in which Umberto Eco had an article. Even if they got my name wrong. No, especially if they got my name wrong!

I got all the friends that money can buy, so I never have to be alone...

Shut up, William, Scott barked. Just...shut...up. Please.

It had been a tense holiday. NASDAQ had tanked completely in the days leading up to Xmas and Scott had lost a bundle. Unknownhypertext.com had briefly flirted with penny stock status, but now you couldn't buy a share, even if you wanted to. After NASDAQ had stopped trading our stock, whatever miniscule value remained vanished. I keep saying "our," as if I had a true stake in the success or failure of unknownhypertext.com. Sure, I got my block during the IPO, but I had nothing before I got the stock, so having nothing now is no different. Only Scott took advantage of the extremely generous options. He kept urging us to buy more and more Unknown stock, "If the creators of the product don't believe enough in their work to invest in it, why should anyone else?" Everyone ignored him and now he's in debt up to his eyeballs. The margin call wiped him out, and beyond.

In the offices of *Rolling Stone*, William had sat in a waiting room with Blink 182. The band were taking turns reading out loud to one another from Wallace Shawn's *The Fever*. William didn't recognize the band, but he did recognize the text, and rather enjoyed the recital. A woman leaned out of a pastel green door and said to William:

We're going to take your picture. Do you want cool clothes?

William looked down at his clothes and realized they were uncool.

Sure. Cool clothes would be, uh, cool.

He shot a brief glance at Blink 182. Nobody had offered them cool clothes, therefore their clothes must have been cool.

Rolling Stone: So, how do you see the Unknown compared to the British invasion of the Sixties?

William: Well, we're the Beatles, obviously. But more of a post-structuralist Beatles. We're taking on literature as less of a pastiche, more of a ready-made. We're anti-bourgeois, but closet modernists. So, if we can recontextualize the Stones as *Sunshine '69*, The Kinks as *Grammatron*, then it is within the heuristic to reconfigure us as an enigmatic Fab Four, with one of us—Frank— a sort of mythological undead walrus. With Roland Barthes as George Martin... I think that Newspoetry.com can be thought of as the Greenwich Village folk music scene, which flourished briefly, only to be plowed under by psychedelic-cum-classic rock.

Scott fumed.

Dirk sealed the joint with his tongue, concluding:

The Unknown embraces the Groucho-Lennonism of The Firesign Theater.

William stopped strumming and singing and stared blandly at Scott.

Why is it, William mused, that every time we convince Dirk to throw an altered reality banquet, Scott shows up in a bad mood?

Because he knows we'll let him go first, Dirk said. C'mon, Scott, choose your poison.

Scott turns to scowl or protest, but Dirk, for once, is taking control.

Now, Dirk says.

Meekly, Scott headed over to the tableau Dirk had assembled.

As Scott began to slowly pick this pill and that button, Dirk continued a thought everyone had already forgotten.

And I never aspired to messiahship; that was your trip. I'm perfectly happy emulating Santa Claus, capitalism's poor excuse of a god. I give things to people. C'mon, William, you're next...

In L.A. we got great tans but in terrible trouble. Unfortunately, I can't remember how.

My memory is a confused blur of Scott and William and Frank and cocaine and the cops who pulled the van over on the Sunset Strip.

I was driving.

I don't remember what I said to them. Then I was lying on the sidewalk in a pool of my own blood staring up at palm trees (gentle fronds), as the cruiser pulled away.

William was standing over me and he picked my driver's license (expired in the state of Ohio a few years back) up off the sidewalk where the cops had left it, shook the blood off it, and helped me gather my robes and limp to the van.

Inside the van were Scott and Harvey Keitel doing lines off the record cover of the soundtrack of the movie *Grease*. I requested champagne.

Excuse me, man, for I am bleeding. Lighten up my soul a little bit, the leeches upon me. I have given the last crust of my body to ferry with these lads across the cracked, wasted unknown of this land. Through a constant consumption of the holy fumes of lab alcohol did I come forth beneath these dazzling palm trees along this Sunset Strip to be rudely pummeled like a spike into this concrete terrain. Or maybe it was ecstasy with Jello Biafra and Flea. In a Mercedes limo, screaming along beneath stars, stellar stars. Life is so strange, destination Unknown.

Remember those glass birds filled with red fluid which, when exposed to heat, would repeatedly dip their heads as if drinking?

I remember red nightsticks coming down again and again like that.

On me.

So, I thought, nowadays cops have a web-browser in their car, and when they run your plates, they also search the web. And that's how they knew I was unknown and learned I was a psychedelics enthusiast and cult leader. So that's how.

Defenders of the streets, the streets of Santa Barbara.

Unknown you're the only one I can talk to
Unknown I await your observations
Unknown I present to you my used up mind
Saturated in caffeine and digital video
Were it not for your rock and roll energy
I would be enervated thoughtless
An obsequious syntax of action
Twists the lift into drag
Do you die because
You have to or because
You saw everybody else doing it first?
I bought my own imagination
I paid top dollar
An exorbitant calculus whose decelerating
Rate of change was always a curve away
Unknown floated me through the blood neon
    whiskeybars
Entrails of city meat
Here in the middle where
A weedy lot may go untouched
I was hoping she would know
But I have to be true
Forgive me whenever
I wish I had four ears
What can I think of true to say?

Why couldn't the Unknown be more like Marx & Engels?

They were uncompromising and stuck together through thick and thin, exile, excommunication and starvation.

And man we're pretty nineteenth century. For a hypertext.

I'd say the Unknown is a product of the Enlightenment. At least as much Enlightenment as Postmodernism. It was all about the Scientific Man, Collaborative Man, Decadent Man.

Marx and Engels were about immortality, different from celebrity. In fact they hated their contemporaries and discredited them with the most snotty invective. No partying with Plimpton, they would have taken him to task for his liberal promotion of bland poetry through his organ the *Paris Review*.

We should have repudiated and excoriated Plimpton with the pertinacity and perspicacity of indefatigable troglodytes.

Such as the time Federman went to a karaoke bar to denounce us and we didn't even show up because we were off blowing a hooter with our people in Eggo.

Hypertext theorists have only interpreted hypertext in various ways. The point is to change it.

Kicked out of the midwest, constantly on the run from police and landlords, lodged like a bullet in the abdomen of the bourgeoisie.

We should have dissolved the Alt-X International.

Disbanded Eastgate when it threatened to get out of our control.

And sent each other money so we could write our masterworks.

Because we are right and those other fuckers are all wrong.

Sort of like Marx and Engels.

Except Marx and Engels were a Genius towering like a genius among geniuses of the Age of Geniuses and we, we are a rock band, like a mushroom cowering among geniuses in the Age of Postgenius.

But we stuck together to write our epic of Hypertext Theory and none of our kids died of malnutrition and there's something to be said for that and anyway I always saw us as more of a Freud.

In that blinding shaft of yellow light, Dirk sings from the "Gospel of the Unknown," backed by the Kronos Quartet. Dirk sings "Someone's Always Fucking With My Mirrors" and the crowd goes wild. We think the tensions between Dirk's followers and the Secret Service have dissolved in the flaring harmonic murmurs of Dirk's first platinum A-side, but then we feel that the tensions are precipitating again. Chelsea Clinton and Uma Thurman are dancing cowboy style, then ballroom style, right up in the front row. I become suspicious of the intentions of one of the Latin Kings nearest them. (Though Dirk's followers generally, or at the very least "often," give me the creeps, right at this point, I feel a sharp sense of identification with them.) I am torn between my enjoyment of this mass lovefest (Spielberg is just backstage right, visibly beaming at my compadre Dirk) and a fear that things have simply gone too far, that something is likely to burst at any moment. Buddy Guy steps in midway through the song, which, in my opinion, just blows the roof off that joint (or would have if it had a roof, which it of course doesn't). Who could not love each other and all fellow humankind when Buddy is singing with Dirk of the dangers of inappropriately adjusted mirrors and of Cartesian doubt of all known sensory apparatus(es?). It is 11:51. The holographic clock is 50 yards high and the heart chronometer's pounding is drowned out only by the wail of the guitar and the floating noise of amplified violins, violas. Dirk's voice almost sounds like that of a singer.

Then the song is done.

Dirk reads from the "Book of Signs;" a battalion of mimes takes the stage as the musicians exit. Is this really how He intends to end the show, and to end the Millennium? With good intentions, a decent gospel, and a mob of mimes? So be it. They (the mimes) are all dressed in purple (which seems both right and wrong).

They are people of all nations, of all ages, of all hair colors and skin tones (Okay, none of this is, obviously, "all" of anything, there are only fortysome people up there on the main stage, but nonetheless, we're talking about a worldwide diversity type of crowd.) None wears any makeup. Some of them turn out not to be mimes after all, but ballet dancers of the utmost grace.

Dirk's followers mouth the words to his most famous gospel, and the mimes work the movements and enact his pastoral preachings, along with the ballet dancers, who dance stunningly well considering that there is no music outside of the telltale heart. It is more beautiful than Swan Lake. He finishes at 11:59. The holographic clock now fills the whole stadium. Steven Spielberg joins Dirk, as the mimes prance about circling them, kicking up their heels and maypole dancing. Together Dirk and Steven count down from

60
59
58
57
56
55
54
53
52

William is still in a coma. Frank is jumping up and down. We're all on the big screen TV. It's even bigger than the one in New York City on that famous corner which always scares me when I see it at the end of the evening news broadcast. It's Orwellian.

49

48

47

46

Who could not think about time at a time like this?

43

42

41

40

39

The mimes and the ballet dancers form a tight prancing ring that whirls about Spielberg and Dirk. The holographic clock is twice the height of the stadium now; they show a shot from the Goodyear blimp. I think about that. It really was a good year, give or take a few serious injuries and a lot of mileage.

35

34

33

32

Euphoria. Fear of Y2K. Good riddance, foul century of my youth.

30

29

28

Whole lives spent and ended. Geopolitical arrangements so-lidified and removed. Ideologies played out, disrupted, man's inhumanity to man, terrors.

25
24
23
22

There is activity on the monitors next to William's gurney. Frank is laughing uncontrollably.

20

My thoughts turn homeward. My mother and father. My niece and my brothers and sister. My grandparents and aunts and uncles. The children I played with when I was young. The two dogs I knew and my cat. My beloved living and my beloved dead.

18
17
16

That circle around the director and my friend, this strange messiah, seems so tight as to be forbidding, so fast it spins to a blur of purple light.

15
14

Will all the machines simply shut down, whir to a halt? Will we return to an agrarian society? What are people really like "in a state of nature?" Do we really want to find out? Was William's bungie jumping accident really an accident? A suicide attempt? A mur—

12

11

10

I'm feeling apprehensive. Something is wrong. Spielberg looks
panicked. Thirty years on this blasted mound of rock. Men have
walked on the moon, but not on Mars. People are more concerned with their President getting a blowjob in the Oval Office
than the guy with no legs who asks them for change at 8 A.M., in
front of the train station, and they walk by.

7

Here it goes. There's still no cure for cancer.

6

Where will we be in ten years?

5

I can't see Dirk or Spielberg, just a mass of purple palpitating
humanity. The monitors next to William are going crazy. Did
he move?

4

How many people didn't live to see this?

3

What will we do after it's all over?

2

Will I ever have children?

I

What kind of world would they make?

The exploding holographic clock, the fireworks, the champagne bottles, the flying corks, the screams of joy, the mass of purple bodies onstage, the flashing of steel, the flashing of steel, the flashing of steel blades, and Dirk's scream rising above all other screams, not screams of joy, screams of pain. William is up and off the gurney. I are confused. There is the flashing steel, the flashing of dozens of blades. It is played out before my eyes and on the Big Screen. I'm rushing towards it, into it, but it is already too late. Dirk lies punctured, stabbed, bleeding from two thousand wounds. His eyeballs rolling across the planks. A body barely held together, chunks of flesh strewn from bones, meat where there was once a man, forty mimes with bloody hands and faces. A wicked smile and evil laughter. William, in his white hospital gown, is splattered with Rorschach test splotches of Dirk's blood. Dirk, who we knew and loved. The murthered messiah. The poet lies dead. There are screams and screams and moans and screams. We are washed in his blood. There are billy clubs and hands on bodies. There are the sounds of small arms being fired. Purple shrouds shed and tossed into the air, clotted with blood. Discarded daggers with taped handles. There is pandemonium, and then there is weeping.

A shock of calm. Near silence, a gathered mass of humanity, weeping for its collective sins.

That was how that terrible century, the twentieth one, came to its logical conclusion. This is the end of my friend and brother. This is the end of the Unknown. This is the horror. The horror. The horror. And only the beginning of what it would become.

There's going to be those tracks through the snow.

When we begin to write, we are making memories, which will be recreated differently when they are read.

A writer loves a reader, because that is where fulfillment lives. In fiction especially. When you write poetry, sometimes you are intimate with yourself, sometimes you are meant to be speaking out loud. In drama you could not do without others there speaking. You are constantly public. But fiction is you alone and the reader alone. That is what defines it. And makes it so particularly lonely and intimate at the same time.

There is both the story and the story after the story. That mystery of who will interpret. Who will know you, and what will your scribblings become?

That is the substance of the unknown.

APPENDIX

by

William Gillespie

Cybertext, Collaboration, and the Beatles (Take 10)

I'll start with the Unknown.

Our philosophy, while coexisting with the subtle and complex and peculiar and tedious and old-fashioned reasonings of the poststructuralist era as well as fin-de-siecle pre-Y2K-apocalypse Clinton-era America, was more simple: we are writers too. We want to write. We are writers because we write. We have discovered ourselves.

And also: we can write together for fun as well as for practice and even for art. Precisely because we are unknown are we free to write. We will read and write each other's writing, and write each other's and our own criticism until we have forgotten who we are, and the edges of our flesh have dissolved, surrendering us to dissipate in a shimmering ether of spirited collaborative intertextuality. We have all the microcosm a scholar could ask for, without leaving the boundaries of nowhere, the midwestern United States, neither east nor west coasts. Textasy, in short, where we can't help but write. Our every movement sends out ripples across the surface of the text. And we can yell and splash each other and get water in our nose, even though literature is supposedly a private pool held by print publishers and professors. Our recognition will follow our confidence. We walked backward into the canon so it looked like we were leaving. The glazed buzz we wore said we had been to many parties like this one.

We want to write. We are writers too. We have discovered ourselves.

And so did chicken succeed egg or vice-versa.

We had written plays, poems, stories, three-by-five cards, radio theater, criticism, book reviews, and the odd paragraph. We had been playing writing games together for years. We used computers. And so the collaboration of the Unknown, the game, came as naturally to us as to some Little Leaguers slipping on their mitts and heading out to the park to play baseball. There was no need to question whether we should be playing writing games: the point was to plunge in and have fun writing. HTML was mostly new to us: a little harder than a typewriter, and a little easier than Microsoft Word. What was unnatural? Why did the writing game last for far more than an afternoon?

Hypertext. [1]

In June 1962, when producer George Martin first signed the Beatles, he was ambivalent about them. "I've got nothing to lose," he reasoned (Lewisohn 17). In their live audition there was little hint of the inventive chemistry they would later achieve in the recording studio. The Beatles started with a plagiarized sound. They were essentially a live R&B quartet, performing mostly unoriginal three-minute songs with verses, a chorus, and a middle eight, for drums, bass, two guitars, and two-to-four-part harmonies. They were cute and competent and sounded American and wore suits. They were commercially perfect, as if they had come in a can.

In the early 1960s Abbey Road was a two-track studio used essentially to capture live recordings without the noise of an audience. There were few ways to revise the live recording without literally cutting up the tape. In February 1963 ten of the songs on the Beatles' first album (*Please Please Me*) were recorded in the course of ten amazing hours. Later the Beatles could easily spend as much time working on a single unreleased song ('Not Guilty') as they did recording their first album. In October 1963 the Beatles first began to use four-track ('I Want to Hold Your Hand'). Four-track stimulated their imagination such that its freedom would soon become a limitation. They found new ways of using the machines to record more than four tracks. They rigged an eight track machine by synchronizing two 4 track machines ('A Day in the Life'). They removed erase heads from a tape deck allowing them to layer sounds indefinitely on a single piece of tape ('Tomorrow Never Knows'). In October 1964 the Beatles first used the recording studio to record an unfinished song ('Eight Days a Week'), listen to the recording, and finish the song based on what it sounded like on tape, and thus feedback between the collaborators and machines began to shape the composition process. In 1965 the Beatles, George Martin, and attendant engineers, began to tape their rehearsals, perhaps understanding that how they sounded on tape was more important than how they sounded in a room ('Ticket to Ride'). And they began to make habitual use of the four-track. By August 1966 the Beatles had stopped performing for audiences and were learning that while the recording studio could capture their live sound without all the damn screaming, it could also capture the sounds and music nobody had thought of yet. A song could be more than a chord structure, it could be a soundscape of imagined timbres. There was so much that the technology was not designed to do, but nevertheless could. The Beatles, George Martin, a few dedicated engineers (notably Geoff Emerick, Ken Townsend, Chris Thomas), and countless largely uncredited session musicians (including Martin and Thomas) literally broke the rules of the staid Abbey Road studios, explored the potential and limitations of the machines, and made art.

An ordinary cassette has four tracks: left and right stereo channels for sides one and two. Multitracking is a process by which simultaneous, independent sounds can be recorded on to different tracks on one piece of tape. For example, with a four-track tape, you could record the drums and bass of a song on track one, while recording two guitars on track two. Then you could play back tracks one and two while adding lead and backing vocals to tracks three and four. You could then mix those four tracks onto two tracks of another four-track tape, losing some fidelity and rendering those four tracks no longer independently editable, but giving you two new tracks onto which you could add, for example, four French horns and the sound of an orchestra tuning up. This is how *Sgt. Pepper's Lonely Hearts Club Band* was recorded.

The Beatles discovered they could use multitracking to record forward, but also to record down. George Martin describes this process as painting a picture in sound with an infinite palette (141), and as adding layers to a cake (149). Instead of simply recording a song straight through from beginning to end, the Beatles could work on the whole thing at once, by layering bits and pieces here and there. They got over the conservative idea that sounds had to be recorded at the speed at which they would be played back. They learned to speed up vocal tracks ('When I'm 64') or slow down instrumental tracks ('Rain') to create effects. They pushed it. Why not a guitar amplifier feeding back? (the Beatles introduced this rock cliché in the October 1964 recording 'I Feel Fine') a sped-up electric piano solo? ('In My Life') or tape loops? ('Tomorrow Never Knows') Why not an orchestra wearing silly hats? a dog whistle? or twelve pianos (and a harmonium) all playing one majestic chord? ('A Day in the Life') What happens when one uses headphones as microphones? ('A Day in the Life') loudpseakers as microphones? ('Paperback Writer') rotating speakers from Leslie organs as vocal amps? ('Tomorrow Never Knows') Can a guitar sound like a piano? What would singing sound like if sung while the singer were lying on his back? ('Revolution I)' swinging around the microphone on a rope

('Tomorrow Never Knows') or if recorded through a condenser microphone immersed in a jar of water? (one of the songs on *Sgt. Pepper's Lonely Hearts Club Band* was recorded this way, its title either forgotten or purposefully omitted from the record to conceal a flagrant and dangerous abuse of Abbey Road equipment) What kinds of distortion could be created by plugging an electric guitar directly into a recording console instead of recording its amplifier with a microphone? ('Revolution') overloading a microphone amp? ('I am the Walrus') or singing directly into the mixing board without using a microphone? (Martin and Emerick were unable to fulfill this impossible request) The Beatles were trying to think directly onto tape and their production team made it possible. Why not the smell of sawdust? ('Being for the Benefit of Mr. Kite') monks singing underground? guitars like seagulls? flanging? ('Tomorrow Never Knows') Why not a song that isn't even a song? ('Revolution 9') When the machines did something unexpected, the Beatles welcomed these accidents as new ideas (the alarm clock in 'A Day in the Life,' the placement and missing final note of 'Her Majesty,' the chance occurrence of *King Lear* when mixing the radio into 'I am the Walrus,' the rattling wine bottle on the speaker cabinet in 'Long Long Long,' the edit one minute into 'Strawberry Fields Together,' the segue between 'Good Morning' and 'Sgt. Pepper's Lonely Hearts Club Band (Reprise)'). Sometimes they even left important decisions to be made by accident, employing aleatoric methods such as the cut-up technique ('Being For the Benefit of Mr. Kite,' the run-off groove of *Sgt. Pepper's Lonely Hearts Club Band*).

Beatles arrangements evolved from how their band sounded playing together in a room to how an imagined band (for example two bass guitars, lead guitar, electric piano, two drum kits, mellotron, eight violins, four cellos, a contra bass clarinet, three horns, a choir of 16 voices, a performance of *The Tragedy* of *King Lear*, and vocals ('I am the Walrus')) might sound playing together but all in different rooms, or even different universes. Sometimes one Beatle might record all the tracks himself ('Wild Honeypie'), occasionally they might play together as a rock band ('Sgt. Pepper Lonely Hearts Club Band (Reprise)'), but most songs used unique and impractical ensembles (for example drums, bass, tambourine, organ, two guitars, honky-tonk piano, vocals, and about ten guys in white lab coats using pencils to feed tape loops through machines ('Tomorrow Never Knows')). If Sgt. Pepper's Lonely Hearts Club Band were a real band, it would need even more people than are pictured on the album cover. The Beatles recorded songs that couldn't be played live. You can't play a guitar backward on stage, it doesn't matter how good you are. They deviated from their instrumentation and genre as the machines imposed their potential and limitations on the music. They challenged the recording studio and challenged the record. Songs didn't have to be three minutes, they could be long ('A Day in the Life') or short ('Her Majesty'). *Sgt. Pepper's Lonely Hearts Club Band*, an album recorded without silences between the tracks, signaled a decisive shift in focus from the single to the "Long Playing" record album as their medium. Now they were composing song cycles. A song might now be written to complement its context ('Sgt. Pepper Reprise') or refer to other songs ('Glass Onion'). Like jigsaw puzzle pieces, a song could lack closure but add closure to the whole.

As the Beatles started out wanting to record traditional three-minute monaural pop songs for radio ('Love me Do') and ended up composing monstrous two-sided layer cakes (*Abbey Road*), *The Unknown* was a conventional idea subverted by an unexpected interaction with technology. In the beginning we wanted to write a book of criticism of our own writing. While it might be unusual for a trio of unknown writers to create a book of scholarly criticism about their own work, the idea of a book of literary criticism was neither original nor did it spring innocently from our artistic vision. Books of criticism are what professional scholars write: a default genre. As an accessory for the book of criticism we would first publish a book of our poetry and fiction: *The Unknown: An Anthology*. As a promotional gesture for the *Anthology*, we would write a hypertext. The hypertext, originally meant to be a bit of ad copy—at most a publicity stunt for the real "serious" print work—devoured the project. In a late revision of the *Anthology*, I added scenes from the hypertext to the collection of poems and stories. (By the time this revision of the *Anthology* was published, all poems and stories were deemed irrelevant and omitted, except for "The Bland Taste.") When the book of criticism appears, it will be as much about the hypertext as it is about the poetry and fiction in the *Anthology*. In this manner our interactions with machines—computers—and the art those interactions created—hypertext—changed the project we had set out to do into something unknown.

In June 1998 the Unknown agreed to write a hypertext together. Hypertext? We shrugged. We started writing. We found ourselves ready to play baseball in a four-dimensional park. It was impossible even to tell which team we were on or which direction to run. But understand: we were there to have fun. It was Saturday. The drugs were to ensure the momentum of the euphoria. There was nothing but to start playing ball. So we played ball. And Christ was it a long game. We had to send out for more beer. It took two days just to find what we thought was first base. We put a major dent in the Booker's and turned inside out every bag we laid hands on. Worried neighbors would visit and give us things to take the edge off, but they could not take the edge off. It was the edge of a tsunami breaking gracefully with the weight of a freight train. After being forced for so long to walk the narrow passageways of sequential fiction, trained as we were in the art of obsolete literary form, the accumulated weight of untried narrative technique swept us up. And we were cool. We had no idea how to play four-dimensional baseball but seldom had the handful of spectators that dotted the bleachers seen a team take the field with such big smiles. And so we played ball. Rather than try to impose the rules of baseball onto this four-dimensional park, we let the park impose its disorder on our game. And it quickly became too late to figure out the rules, or when the game was over. All we had was an infinite beginning. We had no idea how many innings there were, or when the season ended. We would either agree to put down the gloves and walk away or keep playing until we were desperately embittered with our teammates, since every time we made it to third base, and thought we were on the verge of scoring a run, we discovered that in the distance there was a fourth base, and a fifth base, and a sixth base, and if we ever made it back to the home plate we wouldn't even recognize it, it would just be another base. We were caught in a narrative tidal wave trying to swim. Any dilemma we created we had to write our way out of. Any problem in the text would be difficult to erase or extract, it could only be flooded with other writing. We treated accidents as intentions. Scott Rettberg says that the entire hypertext was "a mistake we decided to keep."

We forgot about the book of criticism. The Web became our canvas. If the purpose of HTML was to organize and clarify information then we would use it to disorganize and further complicate information. We played with links, and tried to subvert what little grammar they had. On the Web, the link did not have a standard meaning more explicit than "find out more about this word or phrase." Whatever a link meant wasn't supposed to pose a contradiction or nonsequitur. On the first night of writing, Scott wrote a scene with the phrase "Up in Conneticut, for that unforgettable barbeque with Thomas Pynchon and Don DeLillo, the details of which we have sworn never to reveal." (sic) ('east. htm') From that phrase I added a link to a scene revealing the details of the barbeque ('detailsofwhich.htm'). The link referring to inaccessible information was intended to instigate subversion. The rhythms and juxtapositions of footnotes, rebuttals, digressions, jump cuts, and commercial breaks found their way into our transitions.

It grew. Our complications developed complications. While our intentions at the outset may have been to write a single seamless collaboratively-authored narrative, the nature of the machines created seams. Authoring was channeled into writing individual scenes (HTML pages / nodes). We would sculpt these building blocks, sometimes one at a time, sometimes a sequence of blocks designed to be put together, and add links to and from them, and thus did the impossible architecture of the fiction evolve. The idea of sequence became exponentially more confused with each new scene. *The Unknown* stopped being a narrative sequence, and became instead a narrative sculpture. We were lifted from our familiar world of causality and working in dimensions we had never before perceived. We were composing fiction differently. Dirk describes the writing process as "like a jazz band with each member taking solos that referred to the previous riffs already laid down by whoever went before us." We started out faking a standard—a sort of chromatic 'Take Me Out to the Ball Game'— but after a few rounds of solos we were no longer in a recognizable key and there was no way to end. We kept playing. The narrative grew branches. We clung to the idea of sequence, and scenes became very short, links on multiple interlocking chains ('milwaukee.htm'). We thought the branches of story might exist in the same narrative plane, describing a single coherent story universe, as with much of the sort of fiction we like in books.

When this aspiration collapsed (were we approaching San Diego from the east? ('kansas.htm') or the north? ('sandiego.htm')) there was a sense of release. The last bridge to our understanding of sequential fiction was swept away in the tidalwave. Our compulsion toward closure dissipated, and that tree of branching narratives became an explosion of multiple trajectories, a haze of shrapnel. Each new scene would now take place not after or before but within. We were adding daubs of paint to a canvas, tiles to a mosaic, cutouts to a collage, layers to a cake, writing down. New scenes accumulated autonomy and began to function less as lead-ins to what they linked to ('tomorrow.htm') or commentary on what they linked from ('creativewriter.htm') and more as works that could stand on their own ('rhyme.htm'). Now, while thinking out from the center where the hypertext began, from the first scene we wrote, where the story actually begins ('unknown.htm') to its possible continuations, we were also thinking in from the world (literature) to the story. We began consciously to pay homage to our influences ('cortazar. htm'), to incorporate existing genres ('musical.htm') and styles ('spininterview.htm'). We brought the known into *The Unknown* as we decided that certain people, events, writing styles, and even texts—should become our own. Why not typing tests? ('typetest. htm') our students' essays? ('fivepara.htm') program notes? ('vienna.htm') The Unknown now became skilled in the art of saying much by saying little, attempting through concise scenes to evoke familiar worlds. Though discontinuous, *The Unknown* doesn't seek to disorient you, rather it seeks to orient you everywhere at once ('inorbit.htm'). Few of the individual scenes are baffling ('gospel1.htm'); it might not be clear which diagetic level they take place on, or when they happened in the story, or who is narrating them, but it is clearly science fiction ('inorbit.htm') or ecstatic ('dirkspirit.htm') or about Beckett ('unnamable.htm') or the desert ('texas.htm'). Like jigsaw puzzle pieces that don't really fit together, *Unknown* scenes had closure but made problematic the closure of the whole.

As links accumulated to and from newly added writing, scenes written earlier became more heavily linked to. New scenes were hardest to find. We wrote several endings ('eighties.htm', 'theend.htm', 'laparty.htm'), but the more developments we added, the more reading paths led inexorably back to the center: the first chapters we wrote. We tried to think of a way to offer the reader explicit reading paths that went against this current. Web design standards dictated that we needed a universal means of navigation, and thus were created indexes in which diagetic levels were arranged according to a color scheme translated by Scott Rettberg from the Chicago Transit Authority subway map. In ascending order of verisimilitude the subway lines of *The Unknown* are Brown for Art ('brownline.htm'), Red for Fiction ('redline.htm'), Purple for Metafiction ('purpleline.htm'), Blue for Documentary ('blueline.htm'), Orange for Correspondence ('orangeline.htm'), and Green for our (real) Live Appearances ('greenline.htm'). From this point on, we knew when writing a scene that it would fall into one of those categories. This taxonomy was based on the writing our exploration of the technology had generated, and further exploration took place mostly along the lines of this indexing scheme. In these indexes we arranged the scenes' title tags in alphabetic order by filename. And thus we created navigation that neither clarifies nor facilitates a clean overview of the contents. *The Unknown* has a search engine but you have to read to find it.

As an authoring tool for fiction, typewriters are designed to capture a take of a story, from beginning to end. The technology does not facilitate revision (changing the text once typed). Electronic writing allows limitless overdubbing and in this manner enables more types of collaborative writing. Revising *The Unknown* took place live on the Web (indeed, much of the revision happened after it had already won an international award (in a tie with Geniwait). Being edited during its publication, *The Unknown* was a sort of rooftop concert. When traveling and writing together we would try to make use of our immediate surroundings ('dac1999a.htm') the way a studio recording might try to capture the acoustics of a particular room. Because most scenes were written spontaneously, because much was written on location, and because we excised very little of *The Unknown*, it was important that the first take be strong. We emailed writing to each other. We visited each other in our respective cities ('cinti1.htm'). We devised ways to work around the limitations on collaboration posed by the ordinary one-person computer keyboard. We took turns writing ('ditchscott.htm'). We wrote responses to one another ('algren.htm'). We included email exchanges ('000912. htm') and chat room transcripts ('chattrans.htm'). We wrote to the Web using as authoring tools portable cassette recorders ('inthecar.htm'), notebooks ('brownread15.htm'), postcards ('postcards/1.html'), water colors ('katie/diary.htm'), hotel stationery ('plimpton.html'), and radio stations ('altxinterview. html'). We abused the equipment: we took portable computers to bars and passed them around ('nicknjoe.htm'). We used our friends as characters ('bleakley.htm') and as largely uncredited session musicians ('unknownclub.htm'). As the Beatles traded instruments and each sang lead vocal on every album, the Unknown would write in each other's styles and from each other's point of view ('laauster3.htm'). As the Beatles raided the sound effects cabinets at Abbey Road, and began using scraps of their own outtakes in their albums, the Unknown plundered our own computers for autobiographical fragments: book reviews ('readgaddis.htm'), new year's resolutions ('newyears96.htm'), letters we had sent each other long before we became our own fictional characters ('aug1496.htm'). *The Unknown*'s weird conflation of fiction and autobiography got weirder. Through simple multimedia it was possible to add recordings and pictures to our work. In this manner we could write a fictional scene about a live reading, record a live reading of the fictional scene, and add the live audio back to the scene. As we began to see how this collision of reality and fantasy was adding up to *The Unknown*, we worked with the material of reality and fantasy to facilitate it. The fantasies became more fantastic, and the reality followed, until we were at Brown University using a digital auditorium to perform a scene I had written, entirely satirically, about giving a reading at Brown University in a digital auditorium ('brownu. htm'). After Brown we added to the scene written before Brown the cassette recording from Brown. Paul Auster has a character called "Paul Auster"? well move over, here's three guys writing fiction about three guys with the same names as them, and there is a recording of them reading fiction about themselves reading fiction at Brown at Brown. Instead of two Paul Austers, we've got four Dirk, Frank, Scott, and Williams. They write half as well but there are eight times as many of them. And the thing is, two of those four facsimiles are real, the ones who were credited with authorship whose ludicrous biographies appear somewhere in the fiction, and the ones whose voices you hear reading the fiction about reading fiction at Brown at Brown wearing suits. But this replication was not wholly motivated by canny postmodern strategy. Although Brown has yet to stock their bookstores with big color posters of us, that fiction about going to Brown was a joke that came true. Be careful what you joke about. We thought hypertext was funny; we didn't know how serious it could be.

With regard to the nature of the technology there is no real cause for comparison between the Beatles and the Unknown. While both groups engaged machines with a playful spirit, attentive to unintended effects, the Beatles worked long hours in laboratory conditions (right down to the lab coats worn by Abbey Road engineers) while the Unknown wrote on the fly in hotel rooms ('fbifiles.htm'), at work ('kendralet.htm'), in the back seats of moving cars ('dac1999c.htm'), and on cocktail napkins at bars ('dec1994.htm'). The Beatles had professional recording equipment and access to any musical instrument of the time. The Unknown had an HP Jornada, an LG Phenom, a Kodak Advantix F300, an IAWA portable cassette recorder, and various ordinary computers. The Beatles were paid, as was a production team who could scarcely be improved upon. The Unknown were not paid for *The Unknown*, nor was our manager Marla ('marla.htm'). The Beatles could call upon virtuosic instrumentalists at will and were seemingly under little pressure to deal with them in a professional manner. The Unknown didn't even get an orchestra in funny hats. We mostly kept day jobs. The Beatles had everything they needed in order to create their best work, with the possible exception of privacy. The Unknown were unknown. We had privacy. We could go to restaurants or ride buses or write in public without being accosted by screaming fans. We still can. But the Beatles and the Unknown pushed the machines. Technical limitations, like all constraints, force ingenuity. State-of-the-art four-track equipment in 1966 wasn't quite enough to produce *Sgt. Pepper's Lonely Hearts Club Band*. In September 1968 the Beatles liberated an unused Abbey Road eight-track machine from storage where it was awaiting minor technical adjustments. Nowadays, recording studios can offer well over a hundred tracks, as many as can conceivably be used. *The Unknown* was meant to be a hypertext novel, and writing was almost all that our machines, programming skills, and bandwidth allowed in 1998. Would *Sgt. Pepper's Lonely Hearts Club Band* be a better album if it had been recorded with twenty-four-track technology? George Martin thinks it might have been, but Geoff Emerick unequivocally disagrees: "We were put on the spot, and that was the sound you made at the moment; you had to put the right echo on, the right EQ, the vocal had to be right. It made things easier in a way, because otherwise there are too many variables, and what's the point? Where do you go? To me, that's why there's no great product today." (Massey 79)

Regardless, part of the beauty of *Sgt. Pepper's Lonely Hearts Club Band* is how well it captures its moment in history: the summer of love, the drugs, the utopian yearning, and the machines.

George Martin's contribution to the music of the Beatles cannot be overestimated. He produced almost every song, played various instruments including piano ('In My Life') and harmonium ('Being for the Benefit of Mr. Kite'), scored almost all the difficult instrumental arrangements ('I am the Walrus'), worked late hours, and even made it possible for Lennon and McCartney to co-author albums when the songwriting duo weren't speaking (*The Beatles*). John Lennon would make surreal requests and George Martin would invent the technical means to fulfill them. Paul McCartney would sing the melodies he wanted the string and horn players to play, and George would transcribe them, "writing the dots" on to staff paper for the musicians. George Martin and Geoff Emerick showed a willingness to overlook the rules of the staid Abbey Road studios to devise unconventional production techniques that in many cases would constitute abuse of the equipment. During the recording of 'A Day in the Life,' 40 classically-trained musicians were brought in to record the orchestral buildup (overdubbed four times for a total of 160 on the finished recording). George Martin recalls the evening: "The Beatles asked me, and the musicians, to wear full evening dress, which we did. I left the studio at one point and came back to find one of the musicians, David McCallum, wearing a red clown's nose and Erich Gruenberg, leader of the violins, wearing a gorilla's paw on his bow hand. Everyone was wearing funny hats and carnival novelties. I just fell around laughing! ....When we'd finished doing the orchestral bit one part of me said 'We're being a bit self-indulgent here'. The other part of me said 'It's bloody *marvellous!*'" (Lewisohn 96-97) The incident is a wonderful illustration of what might happen in a collaborative cybertext studio. I dream of such a studio and its engineers. What kinds of skills or disposition might a cybertext engineer need in order to facilitate feedback between collaborators and machines? How might a cybertext producer coax the best possible performances from the writers? What sort of equipment might a cybertext studio have? What tools might enable collaborative writing? Are there no computers built for two?

Coda:
Salsa, Machines and Friendships:
The Spineless Cybertext Studios

The Spineless Books Cybertext Studio is located in the mountains near Las Vegas, New Mexico. The high desert climate is
temperate, dry and silent save for the occasional thrashing of a
blue jay. Flowers and a sugar-water mixture attract butterflies
and hummingbirds to the A-frame cottage with the networked
production equipment (computers, printers, a tabloid-sized
flatbed scanner, digital cameras, recording equipment, and a
thermal binding machine) on the second floor. There are 1700
square feet of interior space (2000 square feet exterior) and it
is still in need of some finish work. A large indoor planter reuses
greywater and grows food and herbs year-round. At night the
skies are lit up like a celestial Times Square, and UFO sightings
are not uncommon. At first, when visiting writers step out of the
car after the hour and a half drive from the Albuquerque airport,
glance around the mountainside uncertainly, and ask to check
their email, they discover that our only internet connection is
a slow dialup, and sometimes become visibly skeptical. But our
computers are in order, if off the grid, and we have come to
believe that the advantages of isolation outweigh those of being
wired to the distractions of the internet.

Members of the Spineless production team take on different
combinations of roles as circumstances warrant. These are people
who are nice to work with, and good at making the machines ac-
commodate the desires and temperament of the artists. They like
to try new things and develop methods of using the machines that
are unique to each visiting artist. William's role is to facilitate
literature by creating circumstances in which the writers can
give their best performances. This frequently involves cooking

dinner, and his stance on cilantro is unequivocal. Our designer Ingrid works with the visiting artists to perfect their interface (print or screen). She specializes in the nuances of Photoshop, Quark, and Indesign, as well as painting, etching, and print-making. Our sound engineer Paul has built a soundproof booth for recording, although he prefers to set up the microphones outdoors to capture audio with the resonance of mountainside. He is fond of his reel-to-reel fourtrack machine, and sometimes uses it to capture the audio before transferring it to the digital studio to manipulate using Soundforge and other digital sound editing and multitracking tools. Yes we have a piano, and the tuner makes it up from Taos once a year. We have no theramin yet, but a baritone ukelele and a versatile assortment of guitars and keyboard instruments. We have also been offered a Wurlitzer Funmaker Organ, though it is not yet clear how we will get it up the mountain. We sometimes fall back on oblique strategies. It (usually) goes without saying that William, Paul and Ingrid are all writers as well, and are ready to jump in to the text when ap-propriate. Some of our visiting writers more memorable lines may actually have been written by our staff, but we'll never tell.

It sometimes inspires skepticism among computer purists that much of the material incorporated into our cybertexts is hand-painted, performed on acoustic instruments, or even typewritten, but we welcome such skepticism. Our art is content-driven, and our projects welcome collaborators whose primary "axe" is not a workstation. Our cybertext productions tend to have a print component as well as an electronic component, and we draw on artistic traditions as diverse as architecture and printmaking (we do not, however, have a sculpture studio on site). The point is not computers, the point is whatever we are working on at the time. And hummingbirds, butterflies, yucca, Indian paintbrush, juniper, and piñon.

1   I use the word "hypertext" to denote multisequential writing. The use of image, sound, movement, or sophisticated interfaces, is not ruled out but not what I mean by "hypertext." I mean text. But I am not talking about a single discontinuous text. I am speaking of any text, print or electronic, that either has explicit multiple reading paths or no default reading path. This includes a dictionary but not *To the Lighthouse*. This includes *The New York Times* but not "The Babysitter." *The New York Times* does not explicitly structure multiple reading paths, but neither does it facilitate a default reading path, the implied (and usual) reader behavior is to scan headlines in some sections but not others, and not to read from beginning to end straight through from AI to H12. I like hypertext though I do not particularly like the word—I don't see how a word like that can ever become a household word, and the fact that it has the word "hype" in it doesn't do much for its credibility as a literature. Incidentally, my "hypertext" does not include footnotes. I concede that the cognitive action of a footnote can be similar to that of a link, but footnotes are a convention of linear text, and the multiple pathways they offer are cul-de-sacs, subordinate to the thoroughfare of the main text as often indicated by a smaller typeface. A footnote makes it appear as though you have a choice of reading paths but in actuality your choice is whether or not even to read the footnote. Unless you break away from the main text in the middle to read the footnote and then stop.

The end.

Bibliography

Cunningham, Mark. *Good Vibrations: A History of Record Production.* 1998.

Gillespie, William, Frank Marquardt, Scott Rettberg, Dirk Stratton. *The Unknown.* 1998-2001. http://www.unknownhypertext.com

Gillespie, William, Frank Marquardt, Scott Rettberg, Dirk Stratton. *The Unknown: An Anthology.* 2011.

Gillespie, William, Frank Marquardt, Scott Rettberg, Dirk Stratton. *The Unknown: Criticism.* (forthcoming)

Lewisohn, Mark. *The Beatles Recording Sessions: The Official Abbey Road Studio Session Notes 1962-1970.* 1988.

MacDonald, Ian. *Revolution in the Head: The Beatles Records and the Sixties.* 1994.

Martin, George, with Jeremy Hornsby. *All you Need is Ears.* 1979.

Massey Howard. "Revolutionary Recording." An interview with Geoff Emerick. Published in *EQ* (January 2000). Excerpted from Howard Massey's then-forthcoming book *Conversations with Record Producers.*

Unknown, the. Personal Interview. August 2002.

The Unknown: An Anthology

Spineless Books. Edition 2.2. © 20-02-2012. $18.
ISBN: 978-0-9801392-9-7
Text William Gillespie, Frank Marquardt,
Scott Rettberg, and Dirk Stratton

Edited and designed by William Gillespie
Cover Art by Kathryn Gilligan
Author Photo by Emil Schavio

This volume consists of texts from the hypertext novel, *The Unknown*
(unknownhypertext.com), written between 1998 and 2001 more or
less collaboratively by William Gillespie, Frank Marquardt, Scott
Rettberg, and Dirk Stratton. Except: "The Bland Taste" is by Dirk
Stratton. "Cybertext, Collaboration, and the Beatles (Take 10)"
is by William Gillespie.

We gratefully acknowledge the permission to reprint the opening
epigraph from Thomas Pynchon's *Slow Learner* (Little Brown, 1984)
granted by Mr. Pynchon via Ms. Melanie Jackson of the Melanie
Jackson Agency.

This book was previously printed with different contents by an
unknown press.

Distributed by Ingram

spinelessbooks.com / unknownhypertext.com

SPINELESS BOOKS   URBANA, ILLINOIS

www.ingramcontent.com/pod-product-compliance
Lightning Source LLC
Chambersburg PA
CBHW031214020726
47499CB00002B/580